UNDERCOVER RESCUE

BROTHERHOOD PROTECTORS WORLD

PAM MANTOVANI

Twisted Page Press LLC

BROTHERHOOD PROTECTORS

ORIGINAL SERIES BY ELLE JAMES

For Clay
Who doesn't read my books
But has always believed in me
That coach was right
You do have a big heart
And you show it everyday
With family, friends, and community
Along with the compassion and dedication you bring to
your work

PROLOGUE

SHEA KIRKWOOD STARED at the mirror. The dirt and grime didn't obscure her reflection even if the face staring back at her wasn't one her mother would recognize. But that wasn't why she looked. Her focus was on her surroundings, not the disguise she'd been using for the past four months.

A quick glance, moving only her eyes, verified her contact was nowhere to be seen. Past experience had her believing he'd decided the risk was too high to meet up with her. Another option was he was currently too high to care about his promise to give her information. Then, of course, there was the final option that he'd sold his information to someone else for that fix he currently enjoyed.

Which was why, when another cautious look

confirmed the bar had emptied entirely, the two men walking toward the bar held her attention. Both were deeply tanned with dark hair and beards. While their guns weren't exposed, she'd dealt with enough of their kind to know they were armed. The killing look in their gazes transmitted their intention.

Was it possible her contact had not only sold his information to someone else but had sweetened the pot by revealing her name and the many questions she'd been asking? The current circumstances warned her she'd made a mistake somewhere. Plus, it wouldn't be the first time she'd been screwed over by a contact. When you dealt with the lowest of humanity, you got to the point where nothing surprised you any longer.

She'd believed she'd been careful while maintaining her cover. She'd lived in a cockroach infested hole in the wall for the last six weeks, had drank enough watered-down beer to float a navy and squashed any and all less than flattering attempts to get her into bed. One near-violent encounter she'd barely escaped had slicked her belly and skin with a fear that had stayed with her for days.

At the moment it appeared all of her work was

blown to hell and back. Shifting her gaze she took inventory.

The shot glass, now empty of the tequila turning hot and sour in her stomach, wouldn't be much of a weapon. Although it might help get things going her way if she was quick and ruthless enough in her strike to take them by surprise. Not that she'd move in any other manner. If she tried to reach the knife strapped to her ankle, one of the two men would be all over her, probably slamming her forehead against the bar. Same if she went for the gun at the small of her back. Bottles that could be cracked on the bar, giving her a deadly jagged edge, were just out of reach.

For the time being she held still, pointedly ignoring the men who stopped close behind her. Their first mistake.

"You will come with us."

"Do I look stupid?"

"You look like a lying *puta*."

"Now, my mother would be really upset hearing you call her baby girl such a bad name." Her nerves might be jangling, but her heart rate was steady as she turned around and faced the two.

"Does she know you are an American pig?"

The second man grinned, as if impressed by his

partner's creative insult. He also reinforced her conclusion that these two were the muscle and not the brains involved with the latest drug cartel she'd infiltrated.

"As a matter of fact, no." She leaned back, her elbows braced on the bar top. The one on her right, the grinning one, reached into his front pocket and slipped out a knife. Short bladed, but the serrated edge could do some serious damage. "She thinks of me more as an angel."

With a quick push of her forearms, she levered up her legs and used the toe of her boot to kick the one on the right in the balls. He dropped to his knees. The other moved, his knife slashing out. Her palm burned with the slice, but thankfully she'd raised her left hand, leaving her dominate right one free to grab a shank of his greasy hair and slam his face onto the bar top. Blood from his broken nose splattered the surface. She added a punch to the kidneys before tossing his body on top of his buddy. As she turned to run, he managed to snag her ankle, twisting enough that she had to bite down on her bottom lip. Again she felt the slash of a blade down her calf before using her other foot to stomp on the hand, freeing herself.

Limping, cursing the bad luck of her blown

cover more than her injuries, she ran out of the bar.

Two weeks later, she cursed again. Only this time, she did so within the safe recesses of her mind. The situation was bad enough. She wasn't about to compound it by swearing at her commanding officer.

"We're looking out for your best interests, Kirkwood. Not to mention your personal safety," he said.

She might know better than to try and sway her captain's declaration, but that didn't mean she had to like it. All the work, all the hours and hours spent establishing her cover. All the ugly things she'd seen and done. Only to be forced to walk away. Empty handed.

It hammered at her pride. She hated that she hadn't been successful in breaking the back of the kind of scum that focused their operation on high school students. The kind that had lured and addicted her brother.

If Shea had one fear, it was that she would someday face her brother while arresting him for drug trafficking.

"I was close, Captain." She stared into a face the same color as rich, dark chocolate. A face she respected and trusted. "Close enough that they're running scared."

"I know."

"Let me go back. I can't just turn my back on what I've done when I'm so close to finding out who's in charge."

"You got too close," her commander said. "We have credible reports that there's a bounty on you." Though she maintained an outward calm, her blood turned to ice. "That's why you can no longer be a part of the operation. It's too dangerous." He shook his head, reached a hand to hover over a pack of cigarettes on the corner of his desk before he pulled back and shoved his hand in his pants pocket. The entire department has suffered through plenty of his foul moods when he finally quit smoking eight months earlier. "Plus, this order comes from higher up on the food chain."

"What order?" she asked, refusing to keep the frustration out of her voice. "Please don't tell me I'll be sitting behind a desk until we identify the leader and get this group off the street? So someone else can step in to take their place," she whispered under her breath.

"As a matter of fact I have a special assignment for you. One that will get you safely out of San

Antonio. The bonus is you won't be chained to a desk and you'll be out of my hair."

Her head jerked up and she met his gaze. "Where?"

"Montana. And," he continued. Her nerves spiked higher when he actually smiled a little. "Your new husband."

CHAPTER 1

SHEA MADE no apologies for having to look on a map to discover where Montana stood in the good old USA. The fact that is was north, way north, of San Antonio should have given her a clue.

Even as her temper flared, she shivered. She'd seriously underestimated the cold.

She might be in this unholy frigid nowhere land for an assignment, but it didn't mean she looked forward to the role she'd be playing.

Hunkering down as best she could in the hooded parka she was pretty sure she'd be sleeping in, she surveyed the landscape. Snow-capped mountains with jagged peaks ringed the surroundings. If not for the foot of snow on the ground and clinging to the tree branches, she imagined it would be pretty. God, she missed sand, cactus and the blistering heat of the sun.

It didn't help her frame of mind that she'd been sent here directly from the Captain's office. Without any information or time to prepare. Hell, the Captain had even sent someone to her apartment to pack her a bag. Beyond his name, and the fact that he was with the FBI, she hadn't been given anything of substance about the man she'd be undercover with. The man she supposedly loved enough to have married. Not a single reason why he'd been selected for this assignment. Not even a damned photo.

"Almost there."

She glanced over at Chuck Johnson, her contact with Hank Patterson, founder and leader of the Brotherhood Protectors. Hank had been instrumental in setting up her cover story. Today he was spending the day with his family, so Chuck had picked her up at the airport and was driving her to her destination. During the three hour drive, he'd been very quiet about any details of the assignment.

"How can you tell?" she asked.

"Don't tell me you don't believe it'll be worth it when you find out who's in charge and break up this ring."

Pride prevented her from asking what he knew about the assignment. "When? Not if?"

"From what I've been told about you and everything you've already accomplished, I'm confident you'll shut this down."

She kept her mouth shut, still hiding her complete ignorance about the nature of her undercover role. He glanced her way again. It had been so long since Shea had relaxed enough to experience either happiness or contentment that it took her a minute to recognize both of those emotions in his grin.

"And take it from someone who knows, pretending to be married can lead you somewhere you never expected to be."

IT WAS A GOOD SET-UP. Hardy Sinclair looked around with appreciation at the interior of the home perched high on a mountain side. He knew people often associated this type of elevated location to be an indication of wealth.

In addition to laying the groundwork for the cover story, Hank Patterson's Brotherhood Protectors group had found the perfect blend of rustic and luxurious for this assignment. The floor-to-ceiling windows provided stunning views of the mountains as well as the meandering creek that led to a stone patio with a fire pit that overlooked an infinity pool. A deck circled the back of the house, showcasing an outdoor kitchen, wet bar, and a hot tub that could accommodate twelve. The eight bedrooms and ten bathrooms were another extravagance for one couple and yet an essential part of their cover. As was the expected gourmet kitchen, a second wet bar, media room, wine cellar, and game room on the bottom floor. Then there was the extensive work-out room he intended to use whenever possible.

Waiting in the expansive great room, with its cathedral ceiling bracketed by timber trusses as wide as his shoulders, he took in the long leather sofa. A single red pillow and a plaid throw over the back invited him to stretch out his six foot plus frame and take a nap. On the other hand, he couldn't help but consider this was the kind of sofa a loving couple might make use of on a snowy day.

He had a mental flash of the file on Shea Kirkwood. Intelligent. Steady. Relentless. Stubborn, according to one evaluation.

Attractive.

He lifted a hand and rubbed at the back of his neck.

Her file photo showed hair razor straight past her shoulders instead of the curls usually associated with auburn hair. Her eyes were a soft grey-green, giving her a girl-next-door impression that belied her expertise in firearms and tactical proficiency. There was also a sharp focus within her gaze if one looked close enough. A nose with a slight bump to it, confirming it had been broken before. A jaw that backed-up the stubborn observation. A mouth he'd bet his salary could curse like a sailor or melt a man's thoughts with honeyed words in equal measure.

It would be both easy and difficult to play the loving, attentive husband to such a woman. He, they, would have three days to get to know each other, and learn their roles, before they tested that relationship in public.

"Show time," he murmured when he heard the rumble of an approaching vehicle.

Dismissing the brief idea of waiting inside, he stepped out onto the stone entry. Through the windshield of a black SUV he locked gazes with Shea Kirkwood. Oh yeah, stubborn fit her.

He watched as she exchanged a few words with the driver, exited and opened the back door to retrieve her luggage. Hardy resisted the impulse to offer help. He preferred to keep both of his hands intact.

As the driver of the SUV honked his horn in goodbye and turned around to leave, Shea walked toward the house. Although Hardy had concerns about how they were going to work together, he had a groin-tightening appreciation for the sway of her hips and the stride of legs encased in snug denim. She stopped a foot away. For an instant, no more than the time it took to draw in breath, her stance wavered.

"I have questions," she said, more demand than comment.

"I'll try to answer them."

"You will," she asserted before she stepped around him and entered the house.

Grateful she had her back to him, Shea sucked in a breath and pressed a hand to her trembling stomach. Good God, Hardy Sinclair was sexier than she'd expected. She couldn't recall the last time she'd had such an immediate, and intense, response to a man. Wait, that would be never.

He stood an easy six foot with a strong build beneath the cashmere sweater as white as the outside snow. He had a mass of curly black hair that begged for her hands to sink in and hold on. A jaw rough with growth had her imagining how that texture would feel against some intimate areas of her body. His crystal blue eyes had not backed down from their first glance, nor from her assertion that she wanted answers. This was not a man easily swayed or conquered.

Needing time to settle on her approach, and hopefully calm her sprinting pulse, she set down her bag and glanced at her surroundings.

"Well," she said. "This is one hell of a lot nicer than the cramped, piece-of-shit apartment that was my last assignment."

"Former beauty queen Shea Patricia Andrews Nelson would never settle for anything less than the best."

She swung around, her eyes narrowing. "Beauty queen?"

"Yes ma'am," he said, taking on a Texas accent as he began explaining their cover story. "Miss Dallas, runner up in the Miss Texas pageant." He patted his heart. "That's how we met. I was a judge." He grinned. "Since it was love at first sight, I had no choice but to vote for your competition. It was the only way I'd be able to sweep you off your feet and convince you to marry me."

She wanted to make some quip about settling for weak seconds, but feared that even as adept as she was at lying, the words would stick in her throat.

"What's your story?"

"Heir to my granddaddy's oil business. I'm filthy rich. And smart enough to know that's what snagged your attention."

She took a minute to make sure her voice vibrated with resolve rather than regret. "I prefer working alone."

"That won't work for this assignment."

"Speaking of which. Since when did the FBI request help from the DEA?"

"And since when did the DEA agree to help?" he countered. "Everyone believed we'd have a better chance of going undetected if we crossed departments."

"You still haven't told me what this assignment involves."

He gestured as he crossed the room. After slipping off her parka and tossing it onto the leather sofa, Shea followed, soon coming to a stop inside the largest kitchen she'd ever seen. "We've been married for two years. This is our newest purchase, the fourth home we now own." He opened a cabinet, pulled out two mugs and set about making coffee. She frowned when he added creamer to one before setting it down on the large center island.

"How do you know how I like my coffee?" she asked, ignoring one of the six stools lining her side of the island.

His eyes met hers, stared deep and long. "I not only know how you like your coffee, I know you were born five weeks premature and your mother named you Shea because it means warrior. You sleep on the left side of the bed, your tell when you play poker is you slide your thumbnail around a corner of your card, and while you can swim if it's absolutely necessary it's not something you're comfortable doing. You wanted a cat when you were younger but your brother was allergic, and you somehow manage to call your parents once a week no matter what assignment you're on." His gaze lowered enough that she could see his throat constrict as he swallowed. "You have a habit of sucking on hard lemon candy several times a day when you're not undercover."

Since she had several lemon drops burning a hole in the interior pocket of her parka, she looked away. "It hardly seems fair that you know so much about me when all I've been told is your name."

"Before the end of three days you'll know

more." His gaze lifted and she saw a profound misery dulling his bright blue eyes. Her heart tripped, understanding he meant something more, something darker, than intimate tidbits about him and his personality that were necessary for their roles.

"I just hope it's not more than you can handle," he said.

In defiance of the tiny prick of worry at the base of her neck she lifted her coffee and took a long swallow, staring at him over the rim. "If my captain didn't think I could handle it, I wouldn't have been sent here."

"I was told you were sent here because there were people in San Antonio who wanted to mess up your pretty face."

Annoyance mingled with disgust in the pit of her stomach. She hated, absolutely hated that her cover had been blown. It wasn't the first time, but at least this time no one had been lost. Didn't mean she had to like it any less. It also annoyed her that Hardy knew more about her then she did about him.

"And yourself?" she returned. "Why did you get sent here?"

"I asked. My sister is the one who alerted us to the problem, so I requested the assignment."

"And the problem?"

"A sex trafficking ring. Of children."

Shea set down her mug, pushed it aside, noticed Hardy had yet to touch his. It made her jittery to think of being involved on an assignment with this kind of emotional stress. A closer study confirmed that Hardy Sinclair shared her feeling. "I think I'd like something a little stronger while you fill me in."

With a barely discernable nod, he walked over to the wine rack built into one of the cabinets. Shea had an appreciative feminine moment to approve the fluid grace in his back and shoulders – not to mention a truly fine ass - as he reached up to draw down two glasses to go with the bottle of wine he brought back to the island. She didn't bother to sigh when she realized he'd selected a bottle of her favored merlot.

"How is your sister involved in this?"

"Allison's a third year emergency room resident." Pride rang in his voice. His hands were long-fingered and quickly extracted the cork and poured both glasses. When she accepted the glass he offered, he didn't release his hold. She lifted her gaze to his as a jolt of charged awareness arched between them.

Never, she thought, never had she worked with

a man who tempted her to consider anything more than the assignment. Even when she'd become involved with Richard she never let her personal feelings interfere with their roles in the undercover assignment. She wanted to believe this unusually quick and strong attraction she felt for Hardy Sinclair was little more than the result of over-work and fatigue. Only, she'd never been very good at lying to herself. So, here she was, around this man for less than ten minutes and wondering what he'd be like in bed.

Thorough.

The word immediately came to her. How could it not when he'd already revealed he knew intimate aspects of her personality.

He would apply the same diligent and focused attention on touching her, kissing her. Pleasing her. She saw it now in his gaze, at the way his eyes drew her in, held her. She felt it as a pulse between them, a tangible connection impossible to deny or ignore.

Every minute of every day while she pretended to be his loving wife would take all of the courage and concentration she possessed to avoid any emotional entanglement.

"Your sister?" she asked, then blew out a breath

when the question broke the spell and he released her glass.

"Allison had a patient, a girl around twelve maybe thirteen come in late one night. Based on her experience and training she believed the girl's injuries were the result of having been beaten. She noticed the girl kept giving this skinny guy who stayed close by apprehensive looks. She trembled every time he made a move toward her or demanded answers from Allison about how much longer the treatment would take. As Allison took her time, he ranted that the girl just needed some bandages and maybe some drugs. Even though Allison could read the signs that the girl already had something in her system. He claimed to be her guardian, but Allison didn't believe him. So, she used medical privacy laws as the excuse to get the guy out of the exam area. That's when she succeeded in getting details from the girl." Hardy took a long swallow of his wine, shifted to stare into the distance.

"Just give me the basics, Sinclair."

"Nelson," he corrected, turning to meet her gaze. "Get used to the cover." She nodded. "The girl had been working for this guy for three years, as near as she could remember, and no longer appealed to a certain client, the ones who like them young. She'd been moved up to a different type of client. She'd been beaten because she refused a client who wanted to have anal sex."

Shea swore, softly but with vehemence.

"My sister alerted the authorities. Arrested, the jerk got a sweet deal by telling them about this organization that took in kids, boys and girls."

"Took in?"

Hardy waved a hand. "They entice runaways off the street, recruit some by supplying them with the drug of their choice and then inform them they had to 'work off' payment. He personally handled two that had been sold by their mothers."

He looked so dismayed, far more than she would have expected of a seasoned FBI Agent. Unable to resist, she reached across the island and gripped his hand with hers. He surprised her by shifting so their fingers could link.

"If this happened in Denver, why are we in frigid Montana?"

Her question brought the ghost of a smile to his lips. She didn't like admitting that in the middle of a professional discussion her thoughts could veer for one quick indrawn breath to the very personal, and intimate, speculation of what that mouth would feel like against hers.

"The organization this guy talked about, the

Denver location is one of several pipelines that transports kids to meet a client's needs. They've recently started working out of this area." He met her gaze and she could see the vulnerability had been replaced by a steely determination that had a shiver sliding down her spine.

"We're here to find out who's in charge of this organization and put an end to them."

CHAPTER 2

HARDY WATCHED Shea's face for her reaction. It helped to keep his mind, and some erotic thoughts, away from how her hand felt entwined with his. Of course that left this thoughts free to wonder just how her mouth would feel pressed to his. Or how her body would cradle his as he slipped inside of her. And how his blood would rush while being captured, held, by her until they both exploded with release.

However it was more than the simple jolt of attraction. It was the understanding and compassion in her hold, in the gaze she kept on his. In spite of her tough-as-nails reputation, she shared his gut-churning loathing for the kind of sick animal that would prey on young children.

"And just what would a young, rich couple . . . happy and in love?"

"Baby." He grinned. "You can't keep your hands off of me."

"Sugar," she said, leaning in close enough to have him thinking, hoping, she intended to prove his claim by pressing her mouth to his. "You've got it wrong." Her gaze dropped to his mouth, rose again, humor sparking a light in her gaze. "You're the one with control issues." She waited and when he didn't rise to the bait, eased back. "That aside, why would we be interested in a child porn ring?"

"You're involvement with the pageant industry didn't stop when we married. You're here as a consultant to the upcoming state pageant." He sipped his wine. "We'll also be invited to several parties where the elite in this region tend to gather. We're very popular guests back home."

"And we'll be going to parties because?"

"Rumor has it there's a cabin nearby that houses the kids. Like a halfway house before they're transported wherever they're wanted."

"And I'm guessing some of those elite we'll be meeting are rumored to have a taste for more than fine champagne."

"According to our sources, at least three, two

male and one female, with known interests are wintering in the area." Hardy moved to the refrigerator, drew out two steaks. "Potatoes are over there." He nodded in the direction of the pantry. "Foil also."

He liked that she didn't argue about pitching in; liked, too much, the way her hips swayed as he watched her cross the room. He also liked, again too much, how easily they chatted while they worked together preparing a meal.

"You cook much?" he asked while watching her chop carrots and celery for the salad.

"You mean your research didn't give you that?" she asked, pausing to slip a slender stub of carrot into her mouth. His mind pretty much shut down for a second. "I don't get much opportunity while I'm undercover. Mostly I stick to basic stuff." She grinned. "I make a really good pasta and meatball casserole. You seem pretty comfortable in the kitchen."

"Mom's a nurse, prefers working the late shift. It was learn or go hungry."

"Your father?"

"Dead." He looked up. "Killed in the line of duty."

"I'm sorry. That must have been difficult."

"It was. Especially since his death revealed he'd been a dirty cop his entire career." Disgusted, with his reaction to the conversation as much as to the history, he downed the rest of his wine.

"Top mine off will you?" she asked. "How do you feel about me sautéing some onions and mushrooms to finish off the steak?"

"Sounds good," he answered, passing over her refilled wineglass.

He liked that she didn't press for details about his father, or offer words that would change nothing. He liked way more about this woman than should be possible after knowing her for so short a time. Damned if he didn't feel a kind of intimacy that had often been missing in a lover. If this kept up, it should make their cover all the more convincing.

"You probably know my parents are educators," Shea said. "Well, my Dad became an Assistant Principal when I was ten."

"Hard to skip school when your parents are so close by."

She sent him a quick grin. "You'd think."

"Is that how you developed your skill at getting in and out of tough spots?" He paused. "Or did that come about when you tried to protect your brother from bullies and then tried to save him from his drug addiction."

"You definitely did your research. No," she said

when he opened his mouth. To argue? Apologize? Hardy wasn't sure. Just that she looked like someone who'd taken a punch to the gut.

"But it does make me wonder if you can dig up this much about me, what about the people we're here to uncover," she said. "I think I should read the file you've compiled for me and this assignment. Can't risk tripping up over my own background."

Pressing a fist to her stomach, she looked at him. He saw lingering anguish in her gaze, buried quickly beneath resolve. God he admired the hell out of how quickly she regained control over her emotions. Guided by a force he couldn't ignore, or deny, he drew her close. She stiffened, then she settled her hands on his hips and relaxed with a sigh.

Hardy realized it had been one hell of a long time since he'd held a beautiful woman.

"You're not on your own this time," he whispered. Giving in, he pressed his lips to her temple, then eased back a half step. He didn't need her to discover he had a hard-on the size of a mountain range.

"I'm sorry, Shea, that you've been thrown into this with little to no preparation. I'm sorry that I haven't been cleared to give you more details. The higher ups have decided the less you know, the better your cover will be that you're simply a beautiful woman who had the good sense to marry rich."

"Not knowing the details leaves me at a distinct disadvantage."

"I understand. I wouldn't like it if our roles were reversed."

"But your hands are still tied."

"Why don't we try this for tonight? Let's put aside the assignment. Just for tonight." Unable to stop, he leaned forward, lightly kissed her. "Let's spend time together as simply Shea and Hardy."

"Shouldn't we use the time to prepare?"

"What's the matter? Afraid to be yourself for a change?"

She lifted her chin in challenge to his taunt. He'd expected no less. "I can be whoever you want me to be."

"I want you. Just you."

Heat flared in her eyes, fueling the fire already burning inside him. If he wasn't careful this could get out of hand.

"Think of it this way. If we get comfortable with who we are in real life, we'll be more convincing in the roles we'll be playing."

"Then we should level the playing field." She

leaned in, her lips curved, humor brightening her eyes. "What's your tell when you play cards?"

"Baby, I don't have one."

"We'll see."

He chuckled while he walked over to the wall screen and programmed music. "Vivaldi's Four Seasons?" she asked after the first few refrains from the speakers. While her reaction might have been predictable he gave her points for knowing the composer.

"It makes dinner conversation easier if you aren't singing along with the lyrics." He lifted his glass, took a swallow. "So, what kind of movies do you like?" He watched, amazed, when her cheeks pinked and she avoided his gaze. "No way am I going to let that question go with that kind of response." She said something, low and incoherent. "Excuse me? C'mon, Shea, how do you expect to handle some of the sleazy aspects of this investigation if you can't answer a simple question?"

"Animated." Her head jerked up, her gaze blazing straight into his. "Disney movies in particular."

Her answer was such a contrast to the tone of her voice, at the way she stood with her hands balled into fists on top of the island. He could easily picture her facing down any type of danger.

Including the threat of him making fun of her. It kind of made him sad to think of her having to always be on the defensive.

"I like movies where I can relax and escape. Suspense or drama skirts too close to real life," she said.

"It doesn't hurt that good triumphs over evil or hope overcomes despair." Gently he covered her hand with his, squeezed. In spite of her defense, he was pleased to hear the often gritty and dangerous line of her work hadn't killed off her optimism. "And love wins."

"Sounds like you've watched your share of them as well."

"I had to babysit my sister while mom worked the night shift." He grinned as Vivaldi drifted into the sensual enticement of Ravel's Bolero. "Plus it gave me points with girls in my teenage years."

They continued to toss questions at one another as they prepared and ate the meal. Hardy watched every move Shea made, not only for professional purposes. He enjoyed her; she had a quick wit in reply to some of his comments, strong opinions and used concise arguments without being bitchy to support them. Not that he always agreed. It seemed as if they both depended on words to deflect the sexual tension between them.

Words could only do so much.

Then there were the lapses of silence, brief but potent. That was when he had free rein to imagine. God only knew what he'd do if she made a move on him.

Thankfully, his cell rang before his mind went too far. He listened, noted Shea watched him closely, all but vibrated with the urge to snatch the phone away from him and hear the update. "No." His denial was very definite, a quick snap of tone that stopped the protest on the other side of the call. He kept a steady gaze on Shea, could all but see the impatience burning inside of her. "We were given three days." She nodded. "That's the plan we came up with, that's the plan we stick with. You do your job and make sure you let it be known we're here. Yes," he answered in reply to the question. "We'll be there."

"Well?" she demanded before he could set the phone on the table.

"Just hammering out a few details. There's time to discuss it all tomorrow." He lifted his wine and sipped.

"I don't like being in the dark."

"Then I'll make sure we have a night light in the bedroom."

"Listen here. . ." She blinked. "Excuse me?"

"In our bedroom. I'll make sure we have a night light for you."

Her cheeks went beet red as realization hit. His blood heated with the same fire. With no trouble whatsoever he pictured her on that big lake of a bed in the master bedroom. Naked. Spread. Waiting for him to join her. Enjoy her. Take her.

The sound of the chair being pushed back brought him out of his fantasy. She stood, damn near over him, fury causing her chest to rise and fall in rapids breaths.

"Listen to me you jackass. Just because I'm part of this assignment. Just because I'm used to being undercover and playing a role. Just because you've got such a pretty face." She drew in a deep breath as if bracing herself. "Don't think for one single second that just because this case has a sex angle that I'm going to tumble into bed with you."

He couldn't say which bothered him the most – her indignation at the idea of going to bed with him or the belief that he would use such a method to get her there. The bitch of it was he was pretty damn sure, with all this pent-up sexual tension riding between them, he could scoop her up, carry her upstairs and they'd set the sheets on fire.

He could admit he hoped to do just that. Not

now however. Now, she needed to be taken down a peg. Or two.

"We'll be playing a role," he began, and was pleased with how calm and steady he sounded. "That role of a happily married couple still hungry for each other. That means there will be certain, shall we say, circumstances where we'll need to look the part. In order to play that convincingly we need to be comfortable, you might even say, intimate with one another." Because he was so focused on her, he caught the flicker of arousal mixed with something softer. Longing, he thought. And it was that quick sign of weakness, of an emotional need, that tugged at him. For that reason he softened his tone.

"Intimacy can be more than sex. In fact, it should be," he said.

He walked around the table, stood close to her. "So, yes, we will sleep together in the same bed." He smiled. "You can put a pillow between us if it'll make you feel better." A soft obstacle, easily spanned. "But you'll have to get used to me touching you. And you touching me." He trailed a finger down her arm. The slight tremor, one she tried but failed to control, tempted him. Instead he wrapped a hand around hers, tugged as he turned to the doorway.

"I know a way we can start."

SURPRISE HAD Shea following without protest. That or she'd been lost in a sexual haze. Never before had a man looked at her as if he cherished her as much, or more, than he wanted to take her to bed. For one quick heartbeat, when he spoke of intimacy, she'd faltered. Yearned. No, she shook her head, it had to be surprise. Hadn't she just thought no man had ever before looked at her in that way? Surprise, or perhaps suspicion, was the only excuse for why she hadn't twisted his arm and tossed him to the floor.

She wondered what would have happened if she had. A part of her grieved for the lost chance, another part considered herself lucky to have avoided any danger of a personal entanglement.

At the base of the wide, circular stairway she came to a dead stop. Irritation vanished beneath sheer astonishment, envy and determination.

The home gym rivaled any she'd seen. Equipment gleamed, offered challenges. Weights curled their finger, inviting you to lift and struggle. Mats promised protection when the body landed. One wall was mirrored while another held a television nearly as wide as the wall. The last was a sliding glass door that opened onto a composite deck housing an exercise swim/spa combination. Some women could be tempted, seduced, by flowers or jewelry. Shea Kirkwood preferred exercise and competition. Somehow, Hardy Sinclair had known. Understood. Accepted.

"There are workout clothes in that dressing room." He pointed to her left, and then disappeared into another dressing room. Eager to move and flex her muscles after so much inactivity she changed quickly. While impressed by the size of the room, the luxury of a steam shower and a vanity, she didn't linger over the discovery that the clothes fit her perfectly.

She also discovered how very well Hardy filled out the snug black shorts and shirt he wore. Edgy nerves pricked her skin.

"Equipment or mat first?" he asked, a warrior's gleam in his eyes.

"Equipment."

She wanted the equipment, and the distance it would give her. She went to the treadmill and started at an easy jog. He went with the elliptical. As she started on mile two, her stride quickened. In the mirror facing them, she didn't try to stop watching the muscles in his legs flex, the strength in his arms as he pushed and pulled the handle. Until he released his hold and used his core stomach muscles to power through the workout. That's when she noted his pace also increased. She knew he damn well did so in a bid to goad her into a competition. She found it impossible to resist. He kept his gaze on his own form in the mirror but she caught the subtle curve of his lips as she increased her speed. By time she hit the four mile mark, her muscles burned, her breath labored and a light sheen of sweat coated her arms and fore-head. He, on the other hand, looked hardly winded.

In silent accord they moved to the weight bench. Her entire body quivered as she stood by, spotting him as he reclined on the bench and stretched his arms out vertically, bringing the dumbbells together over his chest before lowering them to his side. Then, oh God, he shifted to a sitting position and curled the weights, his biceps bulging with each movement.

In the past whenever she exercised it had been easy to focus and concentrate. Never before had a workout left her feeling decadent and sensual. It took all the concentration she possessed to resist reaching out and stroking a fingertip over his muscles.

When it was her turn to lift, he braced his legs, as enticing as his arms, and watched her closely as she went through her repetitions.

"Ten more," he instructed.

"You're a sadist," she panted in reply while starting on the reps.

"You had your chance to push me." His gaze dropped to her chest as she sucked in a breath. The bar trembled as she lifted it, held, and lowered before repeating the motion. The entire ten times.

"Water," she gasped when he covered her hands and moved the bar onto the brace. When he passed her the bottle, she downed half the contents in one mouthful.

"Slow down or you'll make yourself sick," Hardy said, straddling the bench at the opposite end, sipping his water.

Ignoring the slow roll in her stomach, she decided he looked much too smug. "I'm not sure what you think you proved. We spent as much time apart as we did in close quarters."

He took a thorough survey of her. Shea fought to hold still. "What would you have done different?"

"Well." She took a sip of water, lowered the bottle to the floor. After taking the band out of her hair and shaking the strands loose, she scooted closer. And had the satisfaction of watching his Adam's apple rise up and down as he swallowed. "What I should have done. In the interest of safety," she added, her voice dropping to a hoarse whisper. "Is give you a hand of support while you lifted the bar."

Slowly, she ran her hands over his forearms, past the crook of elbow, up to curve around the defined muscle of his triceps. She felt the power and warmth, couldn't hold back the shudder of arousal at the thought of what it would be like to experience the full force of that strength in an intimate setting. How it could be used to arouse and excite or soothe and cherish, depending on the mood. She even considered he might be able to do both at the same time.

"Then." She moved her hands to his shoulders, stroking, massaging. "I'd need to make sure you hadn't pulled anything." His eyes were now the dark navy of deepest night. She had no clue why she felt so compelled to skirt this close to a point of no return. She was on an assignment, one that could impact hundreds of lives, not some woman intent on seducing a lover.

And yet she couldn't find an ounce of caution within her to turn away before things got out of hand.

"You're right," he said and she had a quick skip of thrill down her spine at the husky tone of his voice. "I have been remiss in making sure you were safe." He slid his hands up her thighs. The friction of skin against skin ignited a burn inside of her. Especially when those hands continued up, his thumbs within breathing distance of her center. "It's important that, as partners, we know we can depend on each other." He anchored at her ribs, fingers flexing ever so slightly. Her breathing stalled with the idea, the wish, his hands would rise to cup her breasts.

"You also." He leaned close enough that her entire field of vision was filled with his face. "Need to remember." His teeth lightly nipped at her bottom lip. Then, before she'd subdued the raging urge to grab him, she felt herself enfolded, tilted, and rolled to the floor.

Then all she felt, besides fury, was the hard male body covering hers.

"You should be prepared for anything."

His mouth crushed down on hers.

CHAPTER 3

HE COULD TASTE HER SHOCK. Along with the anger. He figured, if he let up any, she'd take a big bite out of him. Instead, he kept her mouth and tongue too tangled with his to give her a chance.

God, she tasted good.

He'd wanted a taste of her from his first sight of her. Hell, he admitted while changing the angle of the kiss, from his first look at her photo. Now, beneath the fury and the lingering hint of their dinner and wine, came a flavor he'd never before sampled.

Hers.

She'd stopped trying to buck him off. Her hands now gripped his waist, pressing him tight against her. She returned each and every one of his greedy kisses, answering all the raging need that swirled between them.

It would be so easy, so damn easy, to strip her. Take her. To let her strip and take him. To sink into her, have her wrapped around him, cocooning both of them in a silken web of need and desire.

In that heartbeat between taking and pulling back, he heard the sound.

"Damnation."

In one smooth move, he rolled away, stood and reached down a hand to haul Shea up. "Hurry." He started for the dressing rooms, dragging her along. "Get your clothes." He recalled what he'd noticed in his room and assumed hers held the same. "Grab a towel and the robe hanging on the back of the door."

She blinked. "What?"

"Someone's coming. We have to move. Quick."

Thankfully she didn't ask any more questions, didn't hesitate. They went into their respective dressing rooms at the same time, came out almost exactly in step. They took the stairs two at a time.

"What are the plans?" Shea asked.

Hardy demonstrated, spreading his clothes in a disarray, as if they'd fallen after being stripped off on the way to the door leading onto the back deck. "Strip down," he told her, pulling his shirt over his head before heading into the kitchen and grabbing up their glasses and the bottle of wine. Pulling out a drawer, he snatched up the gun he'd stored there earlier. He came back to discover her standing still. "Look," he said, keeping his voice brisk and on point. So far, she'd followed his instructions without complaint. "We don't have time for your prudish sensibilities. We've got to look the part of a couple. Now drop those clothes in your hands on the floor and strip off what you're wearing."

Assuming she'd do as instructed, and trying like hell to not get distracted at the thought of soon seeing her naked, he went out to the hot tub. A light dusting of snow fell, the flakes glittering in the subdued lighting surrounding the deck. He stored the glasses and wine on a side table, tucked the gun within reach behind where he planned to sit and pulled the protective cover off. He spun around at the sound.

His mouth went dry at the sight of Shea wrapped in a towel. Clothes littered the deck behind her, a clear image of her stripping as she walked toward him clouding his mind. Her cleavage hinted rather than shouted at a man while her legs were toned and shapely. "I stashed the workout clothes under the sofa," she said. Her chin lifted a little. "And while I'm not a prude, I would appreciate you turning your back while I get in."

He complied. And ground his teeth together when he heard the sounds of displaced water as she slipped into the hot tub. Once he heard the motor send the water churning, he turned, and noticing she averted her gaze, dropped his shorts and climbed in. The hot water seared his skin. Or was it an internal heat at the thought of being close to her? Either way, they needed to play their parts. He crossed to join her on the shelf where she'd settled. Cool as a cucumber, she passed him a glass of wine and snuggled under the arm he lay along the back of the tub. Within fingertip distance of his hidden gun.

"Just so you know." She leaned toward him, the fullness of her breast pressed against him and with a seductive expression as if they were truly lovers. He wondered if she kept her voice low as a show of control or to prevent anyone from overhearing. Either way it was effective. "If you've pulled this stunt as a way to get me naked I can, and will, hurt you."

"Just so you know." He leaned over to skim her mouth with his, felt gratified when her breath caught, even as his blood pounded as hot and fast as the water where they sat. "Ten seconds more and I would have had you naked on that floor downstairs. Willing and eager."

Then, as if he hadn't already heard the footsteps, he quickly turned his head. "If you don't want me to mistake you for a bear, and impress my wife with my shooting skill." He paused and though he hadn't prompted her, Shea giggled as if delighted with the prospect. "You'd best come out from behind that bush and show your face," he finished.

A man around his age came up the steps, his hands loose at his sides, apparently unconcerned about the inherent threat Hardy had tossed out. Two glints of silver flashed against the weak lighting, one around his wrist and one at the finger of his right hand. He had sandy colored hair just shy of blonde, and a frame that would be best described as thin. While he conveyed casualness in jeans and a lightweight sweater, covered by a leather jacket, they fit as if tailor made. He wore all with the arrogance of a man who believed he held the upper hand. Still, Hardy had dealt with enough low-level dirt bags to see beyond the outward shine.

"I'm sorry," the man said. "I was told the place was empty." He glanced to where the bubbling water just covered Shea's breasts. "I certainly didn't expect to come upon such a lovely sight."

Hardy sent a pointed glance toward the house, where the main level was lighted. "And seeing that the house is obviously not empty, why did you come creeping around the back like a thief?"

"I hardly think I was creeping." He slid his hands into the jacket pockets.

"I do." Hardy lifted his hand, revealing the gun.

"Now, there's no need for that."

"Son, I was raised in Texas. I learned how to shoot before I could write my name."

"He's really good," Shea said, infusing pride in her voice. She lifted her glass and took a slow, unconcerned sip.

"Thank you, darlin." Keeping an eye on the stranger, Hardy pressed his lips to her temple. "Now." He signaled with the gun. "You still haven't answered the question of why you felt the need to come around back when it's obvious the house isn't empty."

"I was worried that someone might have broken in and was using the empty house for a party. Kids maybe," he added with a quick curve of his lips.

"So you came around thinking, what, that you could break it up?"

"I know how to handle a bunch of unruly kids."

"Do you? Does that mean you have experience with your own children?"

"No." Again there was that quick curve of lips, this time with a thinly veiled sneer lining it. "I'm more of what you might call an honorary uncle."

"I see. It's an awful big house for a single man. I'm sorry, I don't believe I caught your name."

"Chad Thompson." He inclined his head. "Is it just the two of you alone here?"

"For the time being." Hardy exchanged a glance with Shea before setting the gun down, still within reach but conveying he meant no harm. "We're Hardy and Shea Nelson, from Dallas. We're on what you could call a combination vacation and business trip."

"Ah, my partner, Renee and I were hoping to do the same." He glanced around, sighing with regret. "It would have been the perfect location." He flicked a glance toward Shea. "For business and various social opportunities."

"What kind of business are you in?" Hardy asked.

"Procurement."

Shea shivered dramatically. "Sugar," she said while she nudged a little closer to him. In spite of the circumstances, and the niggling warning he wouldn't dismiss, he enjoyed the feel of her soft skin against him. "I'm getting cold. My skin's about to just shrivel up. Can we go inside and get warm?" she added with a suggestive tone in her voice.

"That's my cue to leave," Chad said.

"My wife and I," Hardy said. "Are attending a party next week. I'd be happy to ask our hosts to invite you and your partner to join us." He rattled off his cell number. "If you're interested text me so I'll know how to reach you with the details." He winked as he wrapped an arm around Shea. "They're not at the forefront of my thoughts at the moment."

"I can certainly understand why not." Chad slipped a hand into his pocket. Hardy felt Shea brace as if anticipating Chad to draw a gun. He simply moved back toward the stairs. "You enjoy the rest of your evening."

"Drive safe." Hardy shot a glance skyward. "Snow's getting heavy."

Once Chad reached the bottom stair, Hardy shut off the jets on the hot tub. He and Shea remained still and silent until they heard the car engine roar to life and then trail off as their unexpected visitor drove away.

"Procurement my ass," Shea hissed. "He's part of it. Don't ask me how I know, but you're not going to convince me that his appearance here tonight is coincidence. I need to do some research."

Hardy shifted, froze when he realized, now that the jets had stilled and despite her having wrapped her arms over her chest, he had a clear view of her pale skin beneath the water. Her legs were long and he saw a dark, inviting shadow at the juncture of her thighs. She started to rise, no doubt with a plan to walk off her irritation, only to stop with her own realization she was naked. Her head lifted and her gaze locked on his.

Embarrassed, aroused, Hardy found no way to push words past his lips. The lips that had already tasted hers, enjoyed hers. The lips he wanted to use to trace every inch of the body so tantalizingly close.

"Same rule as before," she said, but his ego swelled, along with his dick, at the husky tone to her voice. "Turn your back while I get out and slip on the robe."

Remaining silent, Hardy pivoted. And gave her his back.

SHEA TREMBLED.

She wasn't cold, hadn't been cold since that searing kiss on the floor of the gym. She felt pretty sure the memory of that kiss would keep her warm until old age.

Unless she relented and did more than kiss the man.

This attraction between them might surprise her but it didn't worry her. She'd been attracted to a man before, several in fact. That didn't mean she had to do anything more than consider and imagine. She'd do nothing to jeopardize the assignment. Especially now that she'd had contact with sleaze ball Chad. God, she shook her head, even his name had the ring of pervert to it.

"It doesn't make sense."

"What doesn't?"

She spun around, and, contrary to her determination to keep her mind on the job, her breath stuck in her throat. Suddenly, acutely aware of being naked beneath her robe, she noticed Hardy had put on his exercise shorts but not a shirt. She saw now, defined and within reach, the chest and arm muscles he'd developed. The abs that ridged his center. Granted, she'd already seen, and been pressed against, the strength of those muscles. But all of that had been to prove a point, to play a role.

And while she'd resisted temptation before,

easily, she had a sneaking suspicion Hardy would prove to be a challenge.

"It doesn't make sense that Chad." She didn't even try to block her disgust with the man. "Would come slinking around here." She waved at the wide wall of windows where the accent lighting kept the dark at bay. "At this time of night. I don't care what he says about wanting to check out property he'd been told was empty. You can't tell me you believe his half-baked story. It's not as if we're in the middle of the suburbs, or even close to town. He was fishing for something else." She narrowed her gaze at Hardy. "Just how deep is our cover story?"

"It'll hold up."

"Our visitor tonight warns me there's a hole somewhere, one a snake can slither through. One that can be dangerous to our health. I never ignore hunches. That philosophy has kept me out of the line of fire more than once." Unfortunately, one time she'd been the only one who had escaped.

"I'm not suggesting we ignore your hunch. We both need to be careful. I'll check in with my commander in the morning, make sure everything's secure." He approached, stopped close enough that he could lift a hand and graze his knuckles down her cheek.

"You have my word that I have your back."

Dropping his hand, he turned and headed for the stairs. She had the luxury of staring at his very fine ass. "I'm going to shower while you clean up the kitchen. Then I think we could both use a good night sleep."

"Wait a minute. Why do you get the first shower and I'm stuck with the dishes?"

He continued climbing up, but did look at her over his shoulder. "I cooked," he said, as if that solved the issue.

"I helped."

"You made salad. That's not cooking."

"It is in my kitchen," she grumbled when he disappeared.

Still, she cleaned, indulging in half a glass of wine while doing so. Rather than dwell on the image of Hardy in the shower, she went over every word of the conversation they'd exchanged with Chad Thompson. He'd been careful not to give away too much and yet appear open and without a care. But she'd caught the way his hand flexed when he mentioned, bragged, about knowing how to handle unruly kids. Hardy could call his commander all he wanted. She had sources of her own she could tap. Swearing as she remembered she had no phone or laptop, she took a final swipe of the counter, hung up the dish towel and walked back into the main room.

A frustrating ten minutes later she swore again. All of her attempts to locate any electronic device, other than the remote for the television, had come up empty handed. Then, she walked into the bedroom to discover Hardy, his back pressed against the tufted headboard in a creamy ivory, and his chest bare above the sheet covering his legs, tapping at the keyboard of a laptop.

She wanted, oh she wanted, to fling some snarky comment his way. She wanted to demand an explanation for why she was being shut out of so many of the details of this operation. She wanted, and damn him for making her want, to climb onto the bed and use his body to take the edge off of her frustration. Stubbornness blended with pride prevented her from doing anything more than giving him a dismissive glance, easily done since he hadn't bothered to acknowledge her entry. Turning to the armoire, in the top drawer she found an assortment of lingerie, including an emerald nightshirt in the softest silk she'd ever felt. It made her speculate, wonder, what she'd discover in the walk-in closet.

The shower was bigger than the closet in her small apartment. The ceiling mounted shower head, coupled with well-placed shower towers, provided a water massage that eased the muscles that had knotted rather than relaxed in the hot tub. "Little wonder," she mused as she filled her hand with lavender scented shampoo.

Knowing she needed the sleep Hardy mentioned, she dismissed thoughts of the assignment and luxuriated in the water. Afterward, she rubbed in a generous amount of lotion, also lavender scented, before sighing as the silk nightshirt slid over her body. She'd never believed herself to be the type to get spoiled by such luxury. Then again, she'd had little opportunity to test that theory. With a shrug, she decided she'd enjoy it while she could.

Then she walked into the bedroom, frowning with the realization she would be sharing a bed with, for all intents and purposes, a stranger. Granted the bed was large enough that they could get through the night without touching. Still, it felt odd to slip between the sheets and turn her back to Hardy.

It made her ache for things she rarely admitted she wanted.

She heard the faint snap of him closing his laptop. She waited, but he didn't move to turn off the light or settle under the covers. He didn't reach for her.

"I'm sorry," he said in a soft admission. "I'm sorry that they think anyone who met you or spoke with you for more than two minutes would believe you're anything close to the image of a beautiful woman who lived her life worrying about her appearance and luxury."

Her throat closing, she listened as he shut off the light and stretched beneath the covers.

"However, I'm not sorry," he added, his voice sounding professional and yet somehow seductive. "That we're working together." He paused as if waiting for her to say something. "Good night, Shea."

She lay in the dark, listening to his breathing slow, eventually deepen as he slept.

No, he hadn't reached for her. But his words had touched her.

It was a long time before she managed to fall asleep.

CHAPTER 4

SHEA BELIEVED in the importance of being prepared. On more than one occasion knowledge, paired with training, had helped her slip free of a tight situation. She also believed there came a point in time when you put the notes and studying aside and went into action.

She figured that time had come and gone sometime yesterday.

At least tonight they would make their first appearance as a couple at a party given by Hank and Sadie Patterson. She knew other prominent members of the community along with special guests, including Chad Thompson and his partner Renee, were to be in attendance.

She and Hardy had gone over every facet of their cover. She knew the story of their meeting, courtship and wedding verbatim. She knew details about their homes, their hopes and plans for the future. She'd memorized the manufactured along with the real likes, dislikes and idiosyncrasies that applied to both of them. She'd learned more about beauty pageants than she ever – please God – would need to know in the future.

Maybe if it had all stayed on the cut and dry facts – even contrived ones – she might not feel so twitchy. Only there had been so much more than the details needed to preserve their cover.

There had been moments of intimacy. Touches. Looks. Little bits of personal revelations that skirted closer to reality than pretense.

They had challenged each other while working these past days, teased while cooking, and whispered while relaxing in the hot tub. They'd talked while eating in candlelight like the lovers they'd pretend to be. They'd danced to seductive music with an ease that belied their brief acquaintance.

She knew how to fit into a role, how to use it to her advantage. This current one came naturally enough that it worried her.

While she'd worked with a former lover, Richard, their roles had been closer to their real reason for working together. Their relationship certainly hadn't been as suggestive as hers and

Hardy's was now. So she'd work harder, be more vigilant. No way would she let someone else she cared about lose their life because of her.

Just how much she was beginning to care hit home last night, over one of those candlelight dinners, when he'd slipped the ring onto her finger.

Her gaze now lowered to her left hand. And the brilliant three carat diamond bordered on either side by bands circled with stunning rubies.

"My first thought was emeralds."

Shea glanced up to see Hardy watching her from the bathroom door. Her breath caught in her throat at this first sight of him in a suit. The jacket molded his shoulders and chest, tapered along with his waist, while the slacks caressed muscular thighs. She curled her hands into fists. With a grace she'd almost become accustomed to, he walked to where she sat at the vanity, held out a hand to help her rise. Heels brought her nearly to his height. Her heart pounded so hard in her chest she feared she might pass out.

This – the moment, the exchanged looks, the weight and symbolism of the ring, her longing - felt much, much too real.

"Most redheads shy away from red in any form." He glanced down where he continued to hold her hand, his thumb grazing over the cool diamond. When he looked back at her, his eyes were penetrating and seductive. "But I thought the fire and flash suited you."

"You." She bore down on the emotion straining to break free. "You picked it out?"

"Along with this." He held out a hand, the gesture demanding she look down. In his palm was a necklace with a setting opposite of that of her ring. "Turn around."

As she did so, he looped the necklace around her neck. Then his fingers, warm and sure, secured the clasp. He lowered his hands to her bare shoulders as she lifted her face to stare at their image in the vanity mirror. She could almost swear the ruby, as large as her thumb and circled by small diamonds, pulsed.

His gaze held hers, searched hers, as she did his. For the first time in her career she wanted to resign from an assignment. Not because of fear of the outcome, nor of the danger it might pose to her. The feelings this man incited within her were far more dangerous than having her cover blown.

With Richard, she'd made the mistake of believing their personal connection could blend with their professional approach. She'd been wrong. Deadly wrong. It didn't help her frame of mind to admit her actions had been the cause of his death.

His lips curved a little and while some of the tension inside her eased, another kind of ache arose to take its place.

"Don't worry, the agency has them insured."

The reminder - and when on earth had she ever needed one before? – that this was nothing more than a prop helped her break the stare. She picked up the postage stamp size purse and rose, turning to face him.

"I guess that rules out me running away to some tropical island."

"You look stunning, Shea."

"I clean up pretty well." Her smile came easier than she'd have guessed. She ran a hand down the short column of black silk. "I've never before worn such beautiful clothes while on assignment." She sent him a teasing wink. "Watch your step, Hardy, or I might toss you aside and pick out a rich sugar daddy for real."

"Do you ever consider stopping?"

"Undercover?" She looked at him, read his question in his gaze. "I was only kidding." Only, to her surprise, she found herself pausing, seriously considering. "I haven't taken the time to think about it." Not only did she feel she made a solid, if small, dent in the drug traffic, but her contacts enabled her to continue searching for her brother. She refused to believe he'd injected enough drugs to kill himself. "Have you considered giving it up?"

"What else would I do?"

"You mean something other than travel to some of the more disgusting places in the country? Meet people who would just as soon slit your throat as talk with you? Having your sleep haunted by the devastated faces of those you couldn't help?" She looked at him and knew he could see futility and failure shadowing her gaze. "Do you ever worry about losing your humanity? Never seeing your family again?"

"My father came home to us every night. At least the nights he didn't spend with his mistress and my half-sister." Shea jolted at this unexpected revelation. "The only difference between him and the kind of people we hunt for is he wore a uniform and had the protection of law enforcement behind him."

He sighed. "He used people, called in favors for others. And for himself. Throughout my career I've had people watching over my shoulder, waiting to see if I'll follow in his corrupt footsteps."

She thought of how she'd used her contacts to try and locate her brother. But her circumstance was different, she didn't want to gain anything more than the knowledge of what had happened to Joey. How often had Hardy found it necessary to take the hard way in order to avoid any trace of being accused of calling in a favor?

"You would never be like that," she whispered

"Don't confuse me with the role I'm playing, Shea."

"I'm not. We haven't known each other long, Hardy, but we've spent some pretty intense time together. I believe in listening to my instinct and it tells me you would never betray your personal code of conduct and ethics." She curled her hand rather than reach out to him. "Even if you didn't live in the shadow of your father's choices, that's just not who you are."

"I won't take the chance."

With a finality that hammered at her heart, he turned and walked away.

HARDY LIFTED A TUMBLER OF BOURBON, using the movement as camouflage while he surveyed the room. He recognized a few famous faces, spotted the negligent manner of those who'd inherited their wealth rather than worked for it. He had just as easy a time pegging members of Hank Patterson's Brotherhood Protectors.

To everyone attending it looked like a casual gathering of local residents, full and part time, along with the allure of the rich and socially prominent.

So far, Chad Thompson and his partner were a no-show.

Hardy didn't like Shea being out of his line of sight. He wasn't comfortable admitting his unease had little to nothing to do with the assignment.

He tried rationalizing that it was understandable after the intensity of the time they'd spent together. He refused to play back their last conversation before leaving the house. It hit a little too close to the chest for him. She'd surprised him with her insistence that he could never be like his father. A part he'd never examined wanted to believe her faith in him wasn't misplaced.

Instead he focused on the assignment, the knowledge that once they finished here, they would go their separate ways.

They'd done everything but have sex in an effort to become familiar and comfortable with one another. He wondered, for a brief heartbeat, how much longer that restraint would hold. When two strong-willed people had the kind of immediate response to one another they shared, it was simply a matter of time before they acted. So far, they'd relied on other means to ease the strain of holding back.

They'd had arguments, or challenges as she preferred to label them, over a variety of subjects. She had a quick, agile mind that retained every detail they covered, asked valid questions and suggested alternatives he'd not considered. There'd been talks that shifted from the professional into more personal territory. Without either of them giving away too much.

He'd touched her as they worked out, his hands inadvertently skimming a breast or slope of her hip. He'd held her close while they danced, had felt her heart pound as hard as his. Thank God, he'd been the one who awakened first and had been able to escape the bed before she realized he'd been curled around her in sleep.

He knew she strained against what she viewed as a lack of action. It concerned him, made him question if she might go rogue. She'd done so before. And the result had been the death of a fellow agent. An agent, everyone knew, she'd been personally involved with.

He still wanted his hands on her.

"I swear." Shea pressed against Hardy in a way

that made him thankful he hadn't dropped his tumbler. His blood pressure, on the other hand, went through the roof. "Those babies of Sadie's are just the cutest things. Makes me want to have one of my own. Well, makes me wanting the getting part anyway." She giggled and leaned close, nibbling on his ear as she whispered, "Chad and a woman just arrived."

Playing his role, knowing she'd have a thorough idea of how her act impacted him, he shifted, pressing a hand to her lower spine and bringing them close together. Anyone watching them would assume the lovers were indulging in a little acceptable public foreplay. His hand lowered to hover over the curve of her ass.

"How do you want to play it?"

She blinked up at him, surprised by his acquiesce. Then she beamed a smile as she linked her arm with his. "We wait until they come to us."

Shea kept up the act of adoring wife. Truth be told, it wasn't hard.

She still ached for the man who couldn't escape the dark specter of his father's corruption.

She participated in interesting conversations,

luxuriated in Hardy's attention - telling herself that not all of it was for appearances – and sipped delicious champagne. She'd been primed to suggest they make a move when they were finally approached by Chad and the woman who'd kept a hand wrapped around his arm since their arrival.

"Good evening," Chad said. "It's nice to see both of you again." He smirked. Hardy wrapped an arm around her shoulders and drew her closer. She enjoyed, perhaps a little too much, the sensation of knowing she was protected by the man beside her. "Under better circumstances this time. In fact, you look stunning, Shea." Chad's gaze dipped to the ruby at her throat, then down to her ring, and she could practically see him calculating the cost in his head. "It takes a beautiful woman to outshine such stunning jewelry."

Shea glanced at the woman standing beside him. Around mid-forties, lean, with excellent legs beneath the hem of her emerald dress. Her hair – a honey blonde courtesy of a bottle – was swept to one side so it grazed her jaw while the left side curled around an ear. Not only did the style convey a classic sophistication, it highlight the pearl earring matching the strand at her throat.

She looked like a woman accustomed to wealth and all the advantages it enabled. Shea wondered

what Chad saw in her. Unless, she further speculated, it was the social contacts and wealth that
would provide introductions and camouflage for
his criminal activities.

"I can offer the same compliment to your
companion," Hardy said, extending his hand to
Chad.

"Shea and Hardy Nelson," he said. "Let me
introduce my business partner." He stopped and
sent the woman a seductive glance, effectively
pronouncing them as lovers as well as business
partners. "Renee Redding."

"It's a pleasure," Renee said, snuggling closer to
Chad's side when he wrapped an arm around her
waist. "And I apologize for Chad's untimely interruption the other night." She glanced up at him.
"He knows I had my eye on the house and he
spoils me."

"You deserve it." Chad leaned over to kiss the
cheek that blushed pink.

"Aren't y'all the cutest couple?" Shea beamed a
smile at them.

"Isn't that what you said about us before we left
tonight?" Hardy teased.

"Now, sugar, you know I think you're the
sexiest man here." She winked, broadly enough to
include Chad and Renee. "I mean, after all, this is

the first time since we got here that I've been willing to step out of the house and share you."

Hardy lifted a hand and brushed a knuckle along her jaw. Shea's throat snapped shut at the intimate look in his gaze. She had to remind herself that they were playing a role. But, oh, her heart yearned far stronger than was wise.

"I was more than happy to put off hitting the slopes," he said in a low voice that anyone would mistake for the kind of intimate lovers talk they shared.

"Skiing?" Chad asked.

With no effort, Shea shuddered. "I'll stay inside by the fireplace with a hot drink while I pray you don't break a leg, thank you." She grinned when Renee agreed. "In fact, let's get that drink now." Looping her arm through the other woman's she guided them toward the bar.

"I know what you must think," Renee said as they waited for the waiter to fill champagne flutes. "About me being with Chad."

"That you have excellent taste in men?"

"I didn't." Glasses in hand, the two women moved to a corner. "My late husband. Well." She averted her gaze, as if ashamed. "He wasn't always kind to me."

Maybe she was playing a role, but Shea had an

immediate, visceral sympathy. "That must have been difficult for you."

"Chad is so different from Walter." She lifted her head a little and her lips curved in a small smile. "And not just because he's younger than me."

"Oh?" Shea sipped her champagne. "Is he? I didn't notice."

"You're very kind."

"Not always. I can be pretty catty if someone rubs me wrong." She leaned over, once again slipping back into her role as she lowered her voice to a whisper. "I mean, really, some of the women I've met at pageants can be cutthroat."

Renee laughed. "I like you." She lay a soft hand on Shea's arm. "I think we're going to be good friends."

"I'll drink to that."

As they clicked glasses, the men rejoined them. Chad frowned.

"Sorry, Renee, but I'm afraid I have to cut our evening short." He gestured with the phone in his hand. "I got a call saying there's a glitch with the newest shipment."

"Of course." She set down her glass on a side table, then turned to Shea. "It was nice to meet you. I hope we can get together soon."

"Oh, I hate you have to leave." Shea bit down on

her bottom lip. As had happened several times, Hardy seemed to know how to smoothly follow her lead.

"I'd be more than happy to see you safely home if you'd like to stay while Chad handles his business." He smiled. "I would love to have the company of two beautiful women.

"Oh what a wonderful idea." Shea placed a hand on his arm while she leaned over to kiss his cheek. He gave the impression of being relaxed but his arm muscles were rigid with tension. "Say yes, please," she encouraged Renee.

"That's very considerate of you, but while Chad oversees the trucking business I inherited from my late husband, I've vowed to keep an active role in the business." She glanced at Chad. "So I would like to go along and hear for myself the details about what happened."

"I completely agree with your position," Hardy said.

"She doesn't give herself enough credit for being such a strong leader," Chad said.

"Well, shoot." Shea pouted. "No way I can try and talk you out of leaving now."

"Easy," Hardy murmured when they finished with the good-byes and watched Chad and Renee leave.

"What happened?"

"Our new friend was not thrilled when his phone chimed in his pocket." Hardy nibbled at her lip while explaining. "I only caught snatches of the discussion, but apparently the shipment that was due to arrive tonight was delayed. There were questions about product and storage options." He lifted his head, stared into her eyes. "He was not happy with the answers."

Going along with the pretense, and, damn it, because she simply wanted to, she lifted a hand to caress his cheek. She could not figure out what it was about this man that got to her on every level. "He covered it well. Did you happen to catch where this happened?"

"Close enough that Chad said he'd be right out." He drew her closer, again furthering their cover, while also keeping his arms around her. "He called the man Joey."

Shea froze. She wanted to close her eyes, her legs wanted to tremble. Her heart did. Just as her stomach pitched and rolled with dread. The possibility that her greatest fear of her path crossing her brother's had come true made it necessary to take a deep breath. She wrapped her hands around the lapels of his suit. "We have to go."

"It's a common enough name, Shea. What are the chances it's your brother?"

"I have to know."

"Your brother was into drugs, not this type of activity."

"We both know people like Chad use people like my brother and his addiction for their purposes. And drugs are often used to either lure the kids or keep them docile. Didn't your sister tell you how that girl said it's one way they get the kids?" She rose on her toes so her lips were close to his ear, giving everyone in the room the impression that the lovers were exchanging whispered endearments. "Hardy, I have to know." She swallowed. "Please."

He eased her back, stared deep into her eyes. She saw the hesitation there, the question of whether or not she was too personally invested in the situation. She saw as well his inclination to turn a blind eye to anything that smacked of a personal favor.

"I'll follow your lead," she promised, trying not to beg. "I know this assignment is greater than my concern for my brother. I promise I won't jeopardize what we're here to do."

CHAPTER 5

HARDY STARED AT SHEA. Her distress showed plainly on her face and in her eyes. He heard her plea, along with her vow, in her trembling voice. Could feel it in the way her body trembled against his.

Then there was the fear.

Sometimes fear worked for you, sometimes against. Even though she wanted them to leave and investigate, he guessed Shea feared doing so would confirm her brother was mixed up in this business. Would she, in spite of her promise, act rashly, putting the assignment, and the two of them, in danger? What good would it do to go and find out one way or the other? Did he make this decision because someone, this particular someone, asked for a favor? The way his father had so often done.

He pressed his lips to her forehead. And, smelling her scent, feeling her body pressed to his, recalling the taste of her, he considered whether his decision was based on something more than trust or instinct. He also had to consider his own fear. The fear that he would make a mistake that would result in Shea getting hurt. And yet, he found it impossible to resist her request.

"We'll need to go by the house and change first."

She squeezed his arms, but only nodded before she eased back and sent him a dazzling smile that outshone the worry in her gaze. After they returned to the house to change and arm themselves, Hardy plugged coordinates into the vehicle navigation system.

"How do you know where they are?" Shea asked, the first words she'd spoken since she'd pleaded for this surveillance.

"One of Hank's men put a tracking device on Chad's car." He steered the car over the rough terrain of the dirt road. They'd already traveled ten miles from the house and according to the calculations had another three to go. He didn't need to look over at Shea to know she sat with her eyes trained on the horizon. To sense that her every instinct stayed on alert. He eased to a stop when they crept up a hill overlooking the trucking compound.

A chain link fence topped with razor wire, with only one entrance, circled what appeared to be an office building, what appeared to be a small hotel-sized house, one transport truck and a dark van with tinted windows which prevented seeing inside. Lights were kept to a minimum, primarily shining out to the surroundings at the back of the compound rather than on the premise. While light shined in one window of the office, the house stood dark.

"I don't see Chad's car."

"Could be parked behind the house."

Using night vision binoculars, she scanned the yard. Not spotting the vehicle, she took another survey of the property. "I count three guards," Shea said, her voice low, passing Hardy the binoculars. "One on the back of the transport truck, one near the front cab and one standing outside the office. They're armed."

After using the binoculars, he pointed at the far east corner, directly opposite from their direction. "One more." Through the night shadows he could make out a guard house of some sort. And the muzzle of an assault rifle.

"We need to get closer," Shea said, reaching up

to flick the switch so the interior light would stay off when they opened the doors. "We're not going to know if it's Joey or not if we don't."

He clamped a hand on her arm, stopping her from slipping out of the passenger side when the office door opened. In the silhouette of the interior light coming through the open door, two figures could be spotted.

"There they are," Shea said, her voice conveying urgency. Hardy squeezed her arm tighter, keeping her in place.

Before they could discuss possible action, the office door closed, leaving one man behind with the guard. Shea took the binoculars from Hardy, trained them on the two men as they made their way down the stairs and to the driver side of the van.

"I can't tell if it's Joey or not. The height is about right but it's hard to tell coloring or features with this lighting and the distance."

She'd no sooner finished commenting when the guard took two steps back. A shot echoed through the night, dropping the man who'd been in the office.

"No," she said, jerking back in the seat.

Using the toe of his shoe, the shooter kicked the lifeless body. When he went back into the building, two men walked over to each grab a dead arm and drag the body away.

Hardy braced, expecting Shea to jump out and rush down the incline. Instead she sat stone still. Her expression gave away nothing, her hands lay palm up on her thighs. It was such a contrast to the vibrant woman he'd lived with the past few days.

He couldn't imagine what raced through her thoughts. In spite of her claim of not being sure it was her brother did she believe – fear – she'd seen him assassinated? Was she now planning her method of revenge? Did shock hold her in place?

"We should leave before anyone spots us up here," she said, her voice soft but firm.

"Shea."

"You know I'm right. We can't take the risk of jeopardizing the assignment. You need to call this in and see if the body can be located." She swallowed. "And identified."

Now she shifted, looked at him. Her eyes were alive with pity. It didn't matter whether she knew if it was her brother or not. It didn't matter whether or not this dead man had been involved in the trafficking they were investigating. Somehow this dedicated agent had retained enough humanity to feel miserable about a senseless death. He could also see she skated the thin line of holding firm until she had the privacy to break apart. So, he'd do as she suggested and get them back to the house. He'd even call in this development to his superiors.

But he'd be damned if he left her alone.

SHEA DIDN'T BELIEVE she'd just witnessed her brother's death. Her heart refused to believe it.

Granted her line of sight had been poor, a combination of venue and distance. And while she'd witnessed her share of brutality and killing, it still shocked her system. Somehow she'd managed to keep her voice calm while advising Hardy they needed to return to the house. As an agent she understood the necessity of advising superiors of developments as soon as possible. Even through her distress she could admit it still chapped her butt that he'd be the one making the call to update the situation and discuss future strategy.

Then again she'd never before been so personally invested in an event while undercover.

All these years, she thought and resisted the urge to rock against the cold nerves tap-dancing along her skin, she'd lived in fear of confronting her brother. A part of her, the sentimental sister part, had never really believed it would happen.

The trained agent had accepted, so she'd believed, it was just a matter of time.

When Hardy parked inside the garage, she took a careful breath before she opened her door and stepped out of the SUV. Taking it slow she felt bolstered when her legs held and she made her way into the kitchen.

"Would you rather I not listen in on your call?" she asked, unsure what she wanted him to answer. She gauged she had just enough control left to manage a status update before she would need to escape into the privacy of a shower. She lifted a brow when Hardy swore. Then, she felt the breath crushed out of her when he swept her into his arms.

"Lean on me," he murmured as he brushed his lips, so gently, over hers.

And just like that, she wrapped her arms around his neck and leaned into him.

Whenever Shea had thought about being with Hardy – and God knew she'd thought about it more than she was comfortable admitting – she'd imagined they'd tear at one another, desperate to set off the explosion of desire. To burn away this incessant throbbing need. It's what she'd thought she wanted. Now, however, he opened the door to a new world of sensation.

He cradled her in his arms as if she was precious, caressed his mouth over hers, across her cheek, down the line of her jaw, with gentleness. Tenderness darkened his eyes. Passion did as well. The combination had her heart tripping in her chest.

It's just sex, she maintained as he lowered her to the bed. As he stretched out beside her, his hands running up and down her spine, over her hip. As his mouth continued the soft journey over her face, down to nip at her throat. As his body pressed close to hers.

She didn't care that her shaky frame of mind had been the catalyst. She just wanted to lose herself in the warmth and luxury of touch, taste, and pleasure.

"I've wanted you since you arrived," he whispered. "Staring at me through that truck windshield, pissed off and demanding answers."

Her heart fluttered even as she grinned. "Right back at you." She shifted so she could get to work on his shirt buttons. Only he closed his fingers over hers. Vibrating with lust and determination, she tried to pry her fingers free. He closed his tighter. Frustrated more than annoyed, she huffed out a breath. "I really want my hands on you, Hardy."

"Right back at you," he said, repeating her words. "But, I have to say this."

He closed his eyes, pressed his forehead to hers. Her body turned to mush. So she waited.

"We both know what it's like to want, need, something, anything, to block out the ugly." His eyes opened, looked deep into hers. "I don't want this to be that something."

For the first time tonight, she felt a trickle of fear. She thought about pulling her fingers free, not to work on his shirt but to push him away. What he talked about was more than a way to temporarily sidetrack the thoughts that would eventually come. A way to delay learning the name of the man killed tonight. None of which would be changed by what happened next. None of which would change the feelings building inside of her.

The bottom line was she wanted to be with Hardy. She slipped her hands free so they could cup his cheeks.

"For tonight, for however long we're together, it's just us."

He leaned down to kiss her, a soft kiss that had the sigh rolling up her chest and escaping. "You do that well," she whispered.

He smiled, but there was a dangerous glint in his eyes. "Guess what? That's not all I do well."

"So you say." She slid her arms up to hook around his neck as her body inched closer. "I also have one or two things I do really well myself."

"We'll start with me." His teeth caught her bottom lip, chewed ever so delicately. "Taking what I want."

He took the kiss deeper and while he kept it soft he managed to have her head spinning, her heart pounding. He seemed to be in no rush – either with the kiss or the slow, almost torturous way he undressed her. She wanted to complain that it wasn't fair, she really wanted to feel his skin against hers. She wanted to beg for him to hurry, only his hands – patient, so patient and gentle - had the thoughts vanishing. He cruised his mouth over her exposed skin, tasting, nipping, soothing while he excited. When his tongue took that first long lovely stroke over and into her, her hands curled tight around the sheet as she rode the first climax. He drew another out of her before he made the return trip up her stomach, stopping to taste and torment her sensitive breasts.

That was when she found a measure of control. She tugged his shirt from his pants, skated along the rigid muscles of his back, humming as she welcomed his kiss, as their tongues danced together. She enjoyed the weight of his body bearing down on hers. She thrilled when, as she lowered her hands to slide into his pants and grip his firm ass, she felt the vibration of his groan.

It gave her back the strength his pleasurable assault on her body had stolen. Now, determined to have her way with him, she hooked her legs around him and rolled. She ground her hips, feeling the heat and length of him through the heavy cotton material of his pants as she unbuttoned his shirt.

"Hmmm." She lowered her mouth to kiss the planes of his chest, to nip her teeth over his tiny nipple. "Every time we've worked out I've fantasized about doing this." She skimmed her hands down the center of his torso, hooked a finger into the waist of his pants and flipped open the button.

She slowly lowered the zipper, taking care to not actually touch him. That would come. But she intended to make him squirm a little first.

"Up," she commanded, scooting back a little. When he lifted his hips, she tugged the pants off. Her smile was wicked when she uncovered only male skin and sensuality. A very hard and lengthy sensuality. At the tip was a small bead of moisture, something she'd rarely given thought to before. Now, however, she ran her tongue over her bottom lip. Then, she lowered just enough so her tongue could take a quick swipe over his tip. His cock jumped a little.

"Were you in a hurry when we changed earlier?" she teased.

"Nope."

She lifted a brow at this information. Before she could make a move to touch or have another taste, he swept her up and over.

"But I sure as hell am now." With that he plunged into her.

Her heart stopped, she was sure of it. He cradled her thighs, lifted them so he could sink further into her. Filling her in a way no one before ever had. Lifting her hands, she held on as he thrust over and over. Opposing his words of impatience, he took his time, continuing to kiss, to stroke, to *touch* her – inside and out - while he gave them both the pleasure of sharing.

As she shattered for the final time she had the satisfaction of knowing he did so as well.

When Hardy rolled off her, Shea's first thought was escape. Only he kept his arms around her, pulled her close to snuggle against his warm, muscled body, skimmed a hand down her back. And brushed his lips at her temple.

"Will you tell me about him?" he asked after a little bit of silence.

She didn't need clarification. It may have taken her a second to swallow down the emotion in her throat, but she knew what he wanted.

"Joey was three years older than me. He was a cliché, a chunky kid with hair a brighter red than mine, quiet. With no interest in sports, and even less talent, he took after Mom and Dad, liked reading, excelled in school."

"An easy target."

"Oh, yes."

"You became his protector."

He prevented her from shifting away so she could look up at him. "Why do you think that?"

He kissed her temple. "Because it's the kind of person you are."

"I'm not always nice."

He chuckled, his lips still brushing her skin. "Yes, I know. But you do have a strong sense of right and wrong. It's one of the reasons why I selected you for this assignment."

Pride bloomed in her chest, a pride that went beyond knowledge that she did good work. She'd heard compliments on her work, had numerous commendations in her file. Hardy's simple endorsement meant more. Again, her effort to shift away was met with resistance.

"You're crowding me," she complained.

"No, I'm not. You're trying to escape. I like you here. Now, tell me the rest."

While she didn't especially like being called on the matter, she admitted she did like being held by him. Plus it felt good to talk through old memories with someone who would listen. And someone who, given his past, would understand. It had been so long since she'd felt comfortable enough to expose something so personal. Then there was the fact that she hadn't gotten her hands on his body nearly enough to suit her. She ran a fingertip over his bicep, back up to trace the slope of his shoulder.

"I didn't set out to defend Joey. The first time I came upon two guys shoving him around was the summer before I started high school. There were three other instances before school started. By then I was tired of protecting him, of not understanding why he couldn't, or wouldn't defend himself." She sighed. "As a freshman just discovering boys, I didn't want to start high school with the reputation of being a ball-buster."

Hardy soothed a hand up and down her spine. "Your parents?"

"Of course they were aware. They tried to get both of us to tell them who was responsible, but remember they were the assistant principal and a teacher."

"Neither one of you wanted to be a snitch."

"No. Then, during Christmas break, things changed. Joey said he had some new friends. He didn't come home bruised and bloody. He lost weight. At first Mom was thrilled, then she began to suspect. I, on the other hand, had no clue." She cleared her throat. "Isn't that a kicker? To look back and see what should have been so obvious."

"You were just a kid."

"Hey." She poked him in the ribs. "Ball-buster, remember?"

"I bet you were fierce." He kissed her temple, grazed down to lightly nip at her earlobe.

"I can be now," she suggested, her hand wedging between them, wrapping around his hard length. "Hmm, feels like you're pretty fierce yourself."

"I've been hard and ready since I laid eyes on you." He wrapped a hand around her wrist. "Finish it."

"I'm trying to."

"Shea."

She closed her eyes, but she moved her hand so

she could slide her arm across his stomach and hold him close. "You know how this goes," she whispered. "Joey got involved with the drug crowd. His grades dropped, he began skipping classes. My parents are educators, they knew the signs of drug use. I was shocked, literally shocked when they told me, warned me to keep my money hidden. They searched his room, confiscated his drugs. They tried every rehab available. My mother cried, especially the first night Joey was arrested for possession. A part of me resented him and all the attention his behavior demanded. Still, I tried talking to him. That was the worse." She swallowed. "He told me he thought I'd be happy that I didn't have to defend him anymore. By time he should have graduated, he was lost to us. I've never been able to find him." A single tear slipped down her cheek.

"I was wrong, that's the worse. We have no idea what happened to him." She suddenly pulled back and stared at Hardy. "I've been an agent long enough to know that not every parent gives a damn about what happened to their child. Or, for some really sad reason, not every child wants to go home. But I have to believe that some of these kids we're here to find are hoping to be rescued."

He pressed his forehead to hers. "I'm with you."

He was, she realized. Not just here in this bed, although it was hard to find fault with that little aspect of this assignment. The warmth of his skin dulled the chill of hers. He accepted what drove her, challenged her professionally as much as personally. She knew he fought demons of his own. In defiance of their pasts they'd found a balance together, ready to do whatever was necessary to succeed.

And once they completed this assignment, they'd each go their separate ways.

Ignoring that turbulent twist to her stomach, she slid her arms up to lock around his neck. "Show me."

CHAPTER 6

"Wʜᴀᴛ ᴅᴏᴇs ɪᴛ sᴀʏ ᴀʙᴏᴜᴛ ᴍᴇ?" Shea asked the next afternoon as she and Hardy stopped outside a closed conference room door. "That I'd rather deal with several less-than-savory thugs instead of going inside that room and discuss beauty pageant business with a bunch of women?"

Hardy grinned and drew her close, reminding Shea of how they'd spent the night. And much of this morning. She smelled the soap from the shower they'd shared, felt the firm body that had filled hers. Held hers. His fingers, as they linked with hers, had touched damn near every spot on her body, sometimes in tender stroking and other times in unrelenting demand.

"It says." He leaned down to kiss her, his lips

lingering a moment. "That you're still that ball-buster you were in high school."

She laughed. "Damn straight." She cast a dubious glance at the door. "Not sure that's going to help in here."

"You're the first person I ever requested to work with." She looked back at him, surprised by the sudden turn of conversation. "Because of my father's reputation, I did everything within my power to never depend on anyone, to never ask for anything. I thought you'd understand that. I like knowing I was right." He kissed her. "But then I am often right."

She laughed, choking a little on the emotion lodged in her throat. He was making it very hard to resist wishing they could have more than this temporary relationship.

"Well, with that ringing endorsement I can't fail."

"We can't."

She blinked against the sting of tears as she stepped back and slid a hand down her skirt. "Then, let's see what we can find out."

Several hours later Shea sat with Hardy in a back booth at the Blue Moose Tavern, enjoying drinks, the rustic atmosphere and conversation with Chad and Renee.

"You should have seen her," Hardy said, beaming a smile her way. "She had them eating out of her hand. By time she finished detailing her recommendations, they were ready to do whatever she asked."

"I can't say I've given much thought to the need for security at a beauty pageant," Chad commented.

"You've never been backstage at a pageant. There are all the contestants of course. Then there's wardrobe, stylists, photographers, pageant staff. It's chaos." She shivered. "Anyone could easily walk in off the street and abduct one of the girls."

"Wouldn't they scream?" Renee asked.

"Chaos," Shea repeated, noting how she held Chad and Renee's attention. "Trust me, some of those girls freak out over the littlest thing." She narrowed her eyes. "The greatest danger is the younger contestants. So many of them, this is their first time competing. You really can't imagine how cutthroat it can be, even at an early age. If someone walked up to a young girl, claiming to be a pageant staff, she'd follow them like a lamb to slaughter."

A WEEK LATER, Hardy cast a quick glance around

his surroundings. He wasn't nervous, at least not about flying down the mountain. No matter how extensive his workload, during the winter he made time at least once a month to hit the slopes. Now, his skis cruised over the powder, cutting angles to hold fast while he made turns, the snow flying up in waves. He had enough confidence in his cover story, and his own ability, that he didn't give Chad following behind him more than a single thought.

He couldn't dismiss the itch between his shoulder blades.

Renee Redding gave every appearance of being what she claimed – a rich widow trying to assert her independence by taking control of her late husband's business. While enjoying the attention of a younger man. Though he couldn't yet discern any reason to suspect her story, Hardy wasn't sold. So far his inquiries about her had given him nothing to act on.

He didn't like the idea of Shea being alone with her. She was a good agent, one who knew how to take care of herself, would know how to handle the situation should something unexpected happen. It helped that he'd watched her slip a small caliber gun down her boot leg this morning. Sitting in an upscale chalet, warming her feet at a blazing fireplace while sharing drinks and gossip with her new friend hardly seemed dangerous.

Hardy still wanted to protect her.

She'd been so sad and vulnerable the night she spoke of her brother. Guilt, he well knew, could haunt a person's thoughts and actions.

So far he'd managed to keep her close. The two of them socialized numerous times with Chad and Renee. They'd been introduced to a circle of people who, according to details provided following his reports, were suspected of being involved with massage studios that were under discreet investigation for possible sex trafficking. He'd made a few speculative comments and innuendoes, implying an interest, but so far no one had approached him directly.

Then, last night while in the company of three such men, battling impatience for something to break the case open, he'd confessed to a period in college when he'd tasted a much younger, innocent girl in his bed. He'd spoken of a fraternity brother who would, with the proper financial incentive, provide such girls. While he'd only indulged once, he'd never forgotten the sweetness of firm, smooth skin, the tiny buds of breasts not yet fully developed and the incredible tightness of being wedged between slim hips. Then he'd laughed at himself and questioned if maybe he'd been thinking about it lately because he didn't like admitting he was getting older. Two of the men had grinned at him in understanding and acceptance, one even going so far as to ask whether or not he'd been with a young boy. His stomach churning, Hardy had replied no but then his fraternity brother had only provided young girls.

Later in the evening, he'd noted one of those men having a whispered conversation with Chad.

After they'd returned to their house, he'd related the conversation to Shea. She'd said nothing, and by doing so, by simply holding him close and not attempting to placate, had soothed away his revulsion for his tactics.

When a sudden crack boomed in the sky, Hardy realized he'd glided close to the tree-line during his musings. Quick reflexes had him cutting sharply to the left, enabling him to narrowly miss the falling branch smacking him square in the face. The movement however had his skis sliding out from under him. His body crashed to the ground with a hard bounce. "Shit," he snarled when he felt his shoulder pop out of the joint as he then rolled several more yards downhill.

SIPPING FROM A FLUTE OF CHAMPAGNE, Shea decided this is why certain people traded ethics and morality for the rich life. Granted, she was only doing so because she and Hardy were using the lifestyle and house as cover. Just as, for the past week, she had the thrill of having a talented and attentive lover.

She'd been surprised yet pleased when he started including her in the calls to his superiors since the night of the shooting. It also concerned her. She was becoming far too used to being with him, working with him. She found it harder and harder to distance her emotions and concentrate on the assignment.

She worried that she'd leave more than a plush lifestyle behind once they completed the job and went their separate ways.

Knowing she needed to focus, she glanced around the lodge. Following the cover she'd set-up, she and Renee Redding had stayed behind while Hardy and Chad had taken to the slopes. Even if she had the slightest interest in being outside in the freezing cold – and she figured that was never going to happen - there was something to be said for relaxing in plush surroundings while wearing fabulous clothes and enjoying excellent food and drink. Then there was the company. Renee, she discovered, was well-read and an entertaining conversationalist. Somehow, beneath the gloss of elegance and wealth, she maintained a certain air of innocence that Shea found charming.

She didn't want to believe the woman was involved in the child sex ring she and Hardy had come here to bust apart. But she knew only too well how people hid behind the image they wanted others to see.

"Is everything all right?"

Shea blinked, saw the way Renee studied her. "Yes, of course."

"You look worried." She leaned forward a little, as if in confidence. "You and Hardy didn't have an argument did you?"

"No." Her body heated with the unbidden images of their morning exercise routine leading to a steamy encounter in the shower. Ignoring her trepidation about their time together diminishing, she shot the other woman a wicked smile. "Trust me, we are not fighting."

"I'm glad." Renee smoothed fingers over the crease of her ivory slacks. "My first husband." Her lips flattened and her eyes clouded. "He had a habit of picking arguments with me. He never hit me, but he always called me stupid or unsophisticated. Then he'd use that as his excuse for being with someone else. I found out later," she whispered as she lowered her gaze to her lap as if embarrassed. "Sometimes he was with young girls." Shea covered her hand with her own. The hand beneath hers didn't tremble, instead it felt rock solid. "That's why what you said last week? About how easy it would be to take a young contestant. Well, I admit I've had some bad moments thinking about that kind of thing happening."

"I'm sorry if I upset you."

Renee shrugged. She looked ready to say more, only both of them turned toward the door when a young man in a brilliant blue parka ran inside.

"Clear the way. Someone's been hurt."

Instinct had Shea rushing forward, only to draw up short when Hardy, slumped against Chad, who had his arm hooked around his shoulders, came into the lodge. The feeling in her legs drained away with the blood in her cheeks. She honestly didn't know what she would have done only, at the exact moment she nearly collapsed, Hardy looked over and their gazes met. Strengthened by the resolve she spotted there, she hurried across the room. She also saw his warning to remember her role and not take over like an agent-in-charge, which she answered with a small nod. So, with a quickly indrawn breath, she put a shake, along with some unshed tears, in her voice.

"Oh my God, Hardy. What happened to you?"

"I took a tumble."

"What? But you never fall."

He looked pale, she could see now that she was closer. And a fine sheen of sweat dotted his hairline. She didn't have to work so hard to put that shake in her voice now.

"Are you hurt?" She went to his other side, reached to wrap his arm around her shoulder. She jerked back when he moaned.

"Shoulder," he gritted out. "Came out of the socket when I hit the ground."

She winced in sympathy. She'd once popped her shoulder throwing out a runner at third base during a high school softball game. She'd never forgotten the scream of pain. Adding insult to injury, the third baseman tagged the runner late, resulting in a call of safe.

"He rolled about forty yards," Chad said. "When I reached him he refused to go to the doctor. Asked me to pop the shoulder back in." Chad led Hardy over to a sofa, eased him down. "I still think he should have a doctor look at it."

"Done it before," Hardy said. "Need some ice

and some rest." He sent her a pleading look. "I could go for a shot of bourbon."

"I'll see to it," Renee said, straightening, she snapped her finger at a waiter, issued terse instructions.

In short order, Hardy sipped his bourbon while Shea gently pressed a towel wrapped ice pack to his shoulder. Unable to resist, she leaned forward and kissed his cheek.

"We should go home. You'll rest better there."

He gave her a smile that, while strained, still managed to be charming. "Going to pamper and take care of me, darling?"

"Bet your fine ass I will."

With Chad assisting, and Renee hovering, they managed to get Hardy settled on the passenger seat of the SUV. "Thanks," Hardy told them, closing his eyes as Shea started the engine.

"Are they watching?" he asked as she backed out of the space.

"Yes," she said after a darting glance in the rearview. It surprised her not to see Chad with a reassuring arm around Renee's shoulders. Instead the woman stood ramrod stiff while Chad frowned. "You want to tell me what happened?"

"I angled my skis to avoid getting smacked in the face with a falling tree branch. Barely."

"Why were you that close to the trees?"

"My mind wasn't on what I was doing. I heard a crack and recognized the sound." She chanced a glance over, saw him watching her. "The shot took down a tree branch instead of me."

"Someone shot at you?"

He sucked in a breath when she had to jerk the steering wheel to avoid a rough patch of ice on the road.

"What I keep wondering about," he said once she had the vehicle straightened out. "Is if the target was me. Or Chad."

She didn't like it, not one bit. Yes, she understood Hardy's impatience about this assignment. But his actions had put his life at danger.

Risking another glance, she saw he appeared to have fallen asleep. His color looked better and his chest rose and fell in an easy rhythm. She had a quick, vivid flash of him staggering into the lodge.

Love swamped her so swift and strong she had to squeeze her hands finger-numbing-tight on the steering wheel.

What the hell was she going to do?

Confident of her ability, she'd never before truly worried about her safety while working undercover. That's not to say she was reckless or believed herself invincible. She'd had her share of scrapes, bruises, cuts, as well as evading the hot breeze of a close bullet.

Nothing that had ever been done to her, or the threat of what she'd escaped, hurt as much as acknowledging how close she'd come to losing Hardy today. Oh, she knew eventually she would lose him, knew she would have to learn to live without his steady presence. Live without sharing his bed. But that would be the result of a completed assignment, distance between their two home bases. Not because someone had taken a shot at him.

She couldn't survive going through that again. What she felt for Hardy far surpassed the feelings she'd had for Richard. Which meant it would hurt all the more when she and Hardy went their separate ways.

Chilled, she ramped up the heat so it poured out of the vents.

~

"You can't do this."

"I don't have a choice," Hardy said.

While Shea followed him into the bedroom they shared, he shucked his shirt and went into the big-ass closet. For a second, no more than a single breath, he closed his eyes and searched for calm. For the four days since the skiing incident, he and Shea had accepted every invitation, had been as visible and accessible as possible. They'd again met with the local pageant organization. They were both frustrated with what appeared to be slow, if not outright negligible, progress. Still, neither one of them had considered giving up.

One area where they'd had the most success was their physical connection. He opened his eyes with a grin. It had taken all of eight hours for him to know his shoulder could bear up under the strain of making love to Shea.

They'd also discussed, together and with his superiors, what was the next best course of action. Then, an hour ago, all the attendance at those endless parties appeared to have paid off. He'd received a phone call that, along with instructions to come alone, told him to tell no one where he was to go, and plan on leaving his car behind.

"There's no way you're going to pull this off."

"I have no choice," he repeated, pulling slacks and a sweater from the racks. "I set up my interest. If I ignore or refuse the invitation for this night it'll raise suspicion. I have to follow through." Ruthlessly he suppressed the revulsion. "It's what we came here to do, Shea. To find out who is leading this ring. Going tonight is our first real lead."

"Oh?" She stood with her arms crossed across her middle. "And when they give you your choice of a young girl or boy? When," she continued with brutal honesty, "they watch you, because we both know they film whatever goes on, what will you do? Are you willing to take that young girl or boy and have sex with them – hell, they're sick enough to suggest you have both at the same time - for the sake of this operation?"

"Shea, this could be our only chance at discovering the location here. It could even result in finding out who heads the operation and putting an end to it."

"I know you're a good agent. I understand your need to find a way to stop this ring." She moved to him, caught his face in her hands. "But what will it cost you, Hardy?"

He mirrored her by cupping her face in his hands. His stomach might turn at the thought of what he'd be forced to do in the upcoming hours, but he had to have faith he'd find a way that didn't include the scenario she'd put into his mind. He couldn't think about how his actions might haunt him. Just as he couldn't think about how hearing her concern made him feel.

"What does it cost those kids, Shea?"

An hour later, he reclined with forced anticipation. "How much longer?" he whined in a child's sing-song voice, then laughed.

"You know, Nelson," said a thin man with grey hair at his temples. Chad had introduced them at the ski lodge. "With a wife as gorgeous and sexy as yours, I'm surprised you're here."

"I'm a man used to having what he wants, when he wants," he said with an edge to his voice. He took a shallow sip of the bourbon he'd been offered, praying his stomach wouldn't revolt. Their ride had come with all the amenities - drinks, snacks, porn magazines. And before they'd entered the vehicle each man had handed over a thousand dollars in cash. They'd also been patted down, reinforcing Hardy's refusal to wearing a wire.

"I'm also a man who is always open to trying new experiences." He cast a deliberate, bored look out the darkened window. They'd been driving for nearly an hour. "If we ever get there." He turned back to the group of five men. "Just where are we going?"

"Day care," one of the men answered as the vehicle came to a stop.

Sure enough, when they exited, Hardy saw they

were in front of what appeared to be an abandoned day care facility. There was a fenced playground to one side and cartoon characters now faded from their once bright paint on the side of the building.

There were no other vehicles in the parking lot. While their driver led them to the door, Hardy scanned the surroundings. With little to no street lighting he couldn't make out any identifying landmarks.

"Gentlemen, welcome."

A woman, mid-forties with light brown hair that skimmed the collar of her black suit, stood in a waiting area. Here also the lighting disguised more than it revealed.

"If you'll follow me."

As they did so, passing through a single door, Hardy caught sight of a bank of monitors behind the counter in front of a wide window. Once past the door, there were other windows on either side of the corridor. The woman flicked a switch on the wall and the electronic buzz of curtains opening echoed in the corridor.

"Please." She gestured with a wave of her hand. "Feel free to look and make your choice of entertainment this evening."

With dread hammering at the base of his

throat, Hardy glanced in the first window. A girl, no more than seven and wearing pajamas with fairies and twinkling stars, sat with her thin arms – he spotted the bruising of harsh fingers - wrapped around her up drawn knees in the corner of a wide bed. She rocked back and forth as tears streamed down her face. He caught the red dot of a camera in one corner, confirming Shea's speculation about filming. The next window revealed another girl and, due to the helpless knowledge in her gaze, he guessed her to be closer to twelve or thirteen. A young boy, defiant in the way he stood rather than sat on a bed, waited in the third room. They continued down the hall, passing eight more rooms, all with various ages and genders, including two with mixed pairings.

Hardy watched in silent horror as two men made their selections and entered their chosen room. Make your choice the woman had invited. What the hell choice did these children have? When his phone rang with the familiar notes of The Wedding March, he was torn between relief and fear that the interruption would ruin everything.

"Sorry," he said to the woman frowning at him. "Wife." He pulled the phone out of his pocket, grimaced the way he imagined a put-upon husband would. "If I don't answer, she'll just keep calling." He punched the accept button, but before he could say anything a scream shot through the phone.

"Hardy." Tears and fear rang in her voice, loud enough for the woman beside him to hear. "You have to come. There's someone here."

"Shea? What's going on?"

"Someone." Her breathing was harsh and rapid. "Trying to get inside. You have to come. Please."

"Did you call the cops?" He started moving back to the door, only to stop short when the woman placed a hand on his arm. He shot her a deadly glance. "I'll be right there. Hold on, honey."

"Hurry."

Hardy held out the phone, as if shocked and frightened after the call ended on the other end. "Get me back," he demanded.

"She should call the authorities."

"I'll call them," Hardy shouted, gesturing with the phone in his hand. "I'll call them right now if you don't turn loose of me and get me back."

For one tense, long moment he thought she would call his bluff. "There will be no refund of your money."

"I don't give a damn."

She serenely nodded to the man who'd

appeared at the door. "Take Mr. Nelson back to his car please."

"Hurry," Hardy said, running past the man to the vehicle.

He wanted to encourage the driver to go faster, but figured the guy didn't want to risk being stopped and questioned for speeding. He didn't call Shea back, not sure he could handle hearing anything terrible happening to her while being so far away. Had their cover been blown? Was someone there now, intent on hurting her, because he'd played this wrong? Not waiting for a full stop by the driver, he jumped out and went to his SUV and sped away.

Lights were on throughout the house. "Shea," he yelled as he entered, holding the gun he'd retrieved from the SUV.

"Hardy." She flew down the stairs, into his arms.

"Are you okay?" He tried to set her aside. "Let me check the grounds."

"I'm sorry." Her arms wrapped tight. "I didn't know what else to do. I didn't know if they'd let you keep your phone." He held her trembling body close as he searched the house over her shoulder. "I couldn't let you go through with it."

"What?"

She eased away and he could see now that she wasn't crying. Her gray-green eyes showed more hesitation than hysteria. Still, her chin lifted as if daring him to challenge her.

"I had to find a way to get you away. Before you did something with those children that you'd regret. And live with for the rest of your life."

He pictured the faces of those children he'd viewed, recalled the revulsion he'd felt. With care, he stepped away, moved to a table where he set down his gun.

"Hardy."

He swung around, grabbed her close, banding his arms around her. He held on, rocking slightly, his face buried in her shoulder. He drew in her clean scent, hoping like hell it would erase the odor of sweat, fear and desolation. And, God help him, he'd only seen those children from the safe distance of a glass window. Shea's arms came around him, her hands soothed up and down his spine. Suddenly he shoved her away.

"You took me away from the assignment?"

"Damn straight. I'd do it again if necessary." She met his stare without flinching. "And I won't apologize."

"You had no right."

"I did what I thought was best."

"Best?" he all but spat the word. "There is no best in this operation." He turned his back to her.

"I know." The misery in his voice, and the way he turned away from her, had everything inside of her wanting to go soft, to be gentle. But that wasn't the way to help him. Not yet.

"You think you're the only one who's dealt with something this vile? You've spent too much time riding a desk, Hardy."

He jerked as if slapped as he faced her, then his eyes narrowed. "That's not fair, you know I've done my share of field work."

"Maybe, but field work isn't always dirty. Try being on the streets the way I have the last several years. I've seen what drugs do to kids, I've seen how low they'll go to get those drugs. I've held babies born addicted to a mother whose only thought was how soon she could get out of the hospital and find her dealer. I've seen the signs of abuse some kids suffered because, while their parent was stoned or passed out, a low-life pusher took advantage. So, don't tell me I don't have a clue about what you saw tonight when I've lived it near every damn day."

"Our jobs suck."

"Sometimes." When his shoulders slumped she knew the misery had been set aside. Not extinguished, but put into perspective so that the healing could begin. She took a tentative step forward. "Hardy. I've never had anyone to help me get past the rough patches. Let me be your safety net tonight." She drew in a breath. No one, not the man she thought she'd loved, not even her parents, had ever accepted her, understood her, and supported her as completely as Hardy did. "Then I won't feel so bad about asking you to be mine when I need it."

"There was one ..."

She framed his face with her hands. "Shh." Her lips were tender as they touched his, as they moved over his cheeks, down to his chin. "Not now."

They lowered to the floor. Shea gripped his hands in hers, let her lips coast and soothe. Let them convey the words she couldn't speak. She continued to take him under slowly, gently. Her mouth gave as she guided him away from the harsh reality of cruelty into the soft world of loving. She wanted to show him there were some things in life worth having and cherishing. As his body gave her control, she stripped him, allowed him to strip her. Still she held sway, giving pleasure rooted in love and acceptance. Not once did she allow either of them to lose contact with the other. Here there were no dark shadows, no lingering nightmare. There was joy and sharing. She lavished his body with attention, thrilled when she felt his heart rush beneath her lips, when his groan filled the room. When his hands gripped hers in hard demand.

So the speed changed, the need intensified.

She rose above him, slid down to take him, cradle him, deep within her. Then she reared back, rocked her hips and sent them both flying.

Boneless, with her heart still pounding, Shea let Hardy's strong arms hold her while his body cushioned hers.

"I need to call this in," he said, his voice low.

"A minute more."

"No." He moved his hands so he could nudge her face back. His eyes were no longer angry but they were still miserable. "Let's finish so we'll have the rest of tonight."

So, she sat beside him, her heart aching for the children he described, vile disgust for the men who prey on those children. And outrageous fury for the ones who made a profit from the abuse. Afterward they took a long shower together, using soapy caresses to wash away the rest of the unpleasant. Only for a measure of it to return when they received the call stating the arresting team arrived, after back-tracking through the GPS on his phone, to discover the facility stood empty and barren.

"I'm not surprised," Hardy admitted when the call ended. "Part of their success at avoiding arrest is changing locations and moving kids."

"There's nothing more we can do tonight."

"Maybe not tonight. But I will find a way to stop them." He turned his back to her, punched his pillow. Shifting, she started to spoon against him in the routine they'd developed only to stop when his low vow cut through the dark. "And God help them when I do."

CHAPTER 7

WHATEVER COMFORT she'd given Hardy vanished over the course of the next three days. Moody and withdrawn he went out of his way to piss her off. He worked at a computer late into the night. Shea tried not to think about the images he saw or things he read about.

Unless they were out in public, and even then they'd only gone out twice for form sake, he didn't touch her.

She argued with herself that it was for the best. Once this assignment was completed, and she didn't imagine it would continue much longer, they would go their separate ways. If the assignment ended without busting up the ring, she doubted Hardy would put it aside. He would continue to work angles on his own time. She knew because that's how she'd lived her life for the past few years.

More than the luxury of the surroundings, he'd given her something more in her life these weeks. They'd shared laughter, movies, music, and the pain along with the good of past memories.

With him she'd discovered a softer side of passion, even in the middle of frenzied need. She'd learned how much more there was to receive when you gave without reservation, when you offered everything within yourself with love.

She would miss the hell out of him.

She'd awoken this morning to discover he'd gone out. He hadn't left a message. She spent some time of her own at the computer, coming up with little more than a niggling pulse at the base of her neck. Finally, sick of her own company and determined to do more than wait for direction, she decided to go out. She'd always worked on her own before. No time like the present to start doing so again. With little to go on, she decided to go to the one place where they'd known something had happened. If nothing else, she'd have a chat with Renee.

She dressed carefully, not because it interested her but because she knew it would be expected.

And because that choice enabled her to conceal a weapon.

She considered, rejected and revised strategy while she drove. For the most part she knew she'd have to depend on her instincts. She blamed Hardy. If he'd confided in her more, trusted her more, she'd have a better handle on how to play it. And she wouldn't be approaching the compound on her own.

For a transportation business, the yard seemed quiet. True, there were two semi-trucks parked along the east fence. Surely a business as viable as Renee claimed should have more traffic coming and going as it moved merchandise. Perhaps the lateness of the day accounted for the calm. Once she shut off her engine, she could hear the generator Renee had explained was used to keep the contents of a trailer cool. Staring through her windshield Shea speculated on just what those contents might be.

Studying it in the fading sunlight, she thought it made a kind of perverted sense and wondered why she and Hardy hadn't discussed the possibility before now. The semi could be used to transport children from state to state, hidden behind products listed on the manifest should the truck be stopped for inspection. Plus she knew only too well how often officials took bribes and allowed trucks, in her experience often transporting drugs, to continue on without inspection. The interior could be fitted to accommodate several areas, separated by movable walls. It would in essence be a portable facility, reducing rental costs and easily emptied or moved in case of exposure or an incident such as Hardy's abrupt, and therefore suspicious, departure the other night.

The smart thing to do would be to go back to the house and tell Hardy about the theory she'd come up with.

The door to the office opened and Renee stepped out. With a short wave, she started down the steps.

"This is a surprise," Renee exclaimed when Shea exited the SUV. "What brings you all the way out here?"

While her instincts hummed, she put on her society smile. "You mean I can't just stop in and visit with a friend?" She laughed. "Okay, I admit I do have an ulterior motive."

"Is that so?"

"Yes. You did seem interested whenever I discussed the pageant." She looped her arm through Renee's and steered the older woman toward the office. "I thought with you being a woman running a business. One who's overcome personal difficulty," she went on in a confidential tone. "Well, you're a shining example for the girls in the pageant." She squeezed her arm a little. "I was hoping you'd consider becoming a sponsor for the pageant."

"I'd be more than happy to write a check."

"Well, of course the money would be appreciated. But I was also thinking more along the lines of a personal involvement. You could maybe set-up a mentor program, where girls could observe you in the business world, see first-hand what they can accomplish if they study and work hard."

"I'm flattered you think I'd be an inspiration to those girls."

"Oh, I know you would." She smiled at Renee as they stopped at the foot of the stairs. The steps where she had watched a man be killed. "Maybe you could give me a quick tour of the place so I'd have a better idea of just how you could help?"

"I'm sorry, but I'm right in the middle of something." Renee paused, only to sigh a little. "The profit and loss statement for this quarter. Not at all exciting."

She should have left then, only she hesitated long enough that the sound of tires crunching on gravel drew her gaze. And she watched a vehicle, identical to the one Hardy described he'd ridden in, park alongside one of the trailers.

"You really should have called first, Shea." The arm she'd been holding compressed tight, keeping her in place.

"You're absolutely right," she answered, working to keep her voice light. "I was wrong to think you'd have time for me. After all, as I said, you're a busy businesswoman. I'll just get out of your way. We can talk about the pageant another time."

"No."

She blinked as if confused. "But you said you'd be happy to help out with the pageant."

"And I would have. Now, however, you and I have other business we'll need to settle."

"Business? But, that's Hardy's area. I just give the pageants a little advice now and then."

"You're very good," Renee said. "I have to admit until this very minute I believed you were little more than an empty-headed former beauty queen. FBI?"

There always came a time when you either went with or called a halt to a role. Never would Shea have believed the elegant woman standing before her would have an inkling of what was going on around her. Now it appeared she not only knew but had a hand in the operation.

"And here I thought you were nothing more than a pitiful old woman who believed she had nothing more than her fortune to offer a younger man."

Renee laughed. "Oh, darling girl. Trust me, the money is beyond what you can imagine. I've worked hard for every nickel and dollar. But I have much more than money to offer any man. Including yours."

For a long-held breath, Shea hesitated. Surely she didn't mean she'd slept with Hardy? No. And Hardy had too much integrity to take a bribe. Plus his history would have kept him from following his father's example. She'd seen his fury and misery at having seen those kids at the abandoned day care. She'd held him throughout a night when nightmares plagued his mind and heart.

Furious at the planted doubt, she jerked her arm free and took a step back. Weighing options, gauging her move, she slid a hand toward her weapon only to have Renee clamp down on her wrist hard enough for a slash of pain to radiate up her arm. With her free hand, Renee slipped the gun free just as voices shouted across the yard. Both women looked toward the trailer. Leaving two other men behind, Hardy walked their way. Chad followed close on his heels.

"While," Renee said, "this isn't the sort of social gathering we've become accustomed to sharing during our acquaintance, I believe I can find a way to make it memorable."

"What's going on?" Chad asked.

"Shea was just explaining that I can't hold a man's attention unless it's with my money." She shifted slightly, keeping Shea within her grasp but outside of Hardy's reach. "Would you agree darling?" she asked Chad.

"You know you mean more to me than simply an excellent bed partner." He grinned. "Even though I happen to believe that's one of the best parts of our relationship."

"Yes, you've been an attentive and tireless lover," she purred. "I will miss that part of our relationship."

"Miss?"

"Did you think I wouldn't find out? That I didn't know? Haven't you learned that I always know what's going on with every facet of my business?" Her voice sharpened, as did the look in her eyes as she stared at Chad. "You actually think you could go to the authorities and I not find out?

"Renee."

Chad stepped forward, reaching for her only to pull up short when she held up Shea's gun. Shea looked at Hardy, saw realization crease his features, realized he had somehow brokered a deal with Chad. It had to be why he was here now. And while she could be disappointed, and hurt, by him not confiding in her, she also realized her presence changed everything. She looked away, scanning the surroundings while thinking of the best avenue for either escape or cover.

"I haven't survived this long by depending on anyone but myself," Renee continued. "You think because I enjoyed you in bed that I would trust you? I trust no one. Especially a man."

Shea jerked at the sound of the gun echoing across the yard. And the bright red bloom of blood spreading across Chad's chest. Voices rang out, shouts of identification, calls to put down the gun. Renee pivoted with apparent calm and aimed the gun at Hardy.

Shea could have tried to shove or tackle Renee, hope she moved quick enough to have the bullet flying off mark. But that wouldn't guarantee the bullet wouldn't somehow hit him.

Instead, she moved not with instinct but with love.

She stepped in front of him, felt the burn and pain of the bullet ripping high into her chest.

As if from a distance she heard voices, alternating between loud, rushed, calm. Her body lurched with movement, she felt it rise and settle. Float. She was lifted, moved. There were disjointed flashes of light and darkness. Voices spoke to her but the words were garbled.

Then she heard crying.

When her brain finally shoved aside the floating, when her body began to scream in pain, her eyes slowly opened.

White walls, intermittent beeping, hard-as-a-rock pillow. There was no lapse of memory. True, there might be quick snatches of recall followed by blank spaces, but she knew she'd been shot. Knew why.

"Damn," she muttered. "Hospital."

"Baby."

And there was her mother, tears blurring the green eyes Shea had inherited along with the red hair. Those eyes were lined with worry, shadowed by cautious optimism. She winced, then nearly smiled. If she could be embarrassed about swearing in front of her mother, she must be on her way to recovery.

"Mom, I'm okay." Her eyelids fluttered. "Tired." She ran her tongue around her mouth. "Thirsty."

The ice chips brought relief. As did the soft kiss her mother pressed to her forehead.

"Daddy?" she asked.

"He's downstairs, donating blood. He'll be so happy to see you awake. His little girl," Joyce Kirkwood said, her voice wavering before she regained control. "You're going to be fine. Just fine."

She didn't know, and was positive she wasn't ready to ask, if Hardy was close by.

She didn't ask for details of how she came to be here or anything about the assignment. She didn't ask about the extent of her injuries or recovery. A wound would heal. She wasn't as sure about her heart.

So, for the next three days, she remained quiet while her parents fussed and medical personnel tended. She slept for what felt like hours on end, blaming medication and not avoidance.

Until the day she and her mother were arguing about her returning to work, only to be interrupted by a man who introduced himself as Hardy's supervisor. She learned that while he'd worked to keep her still, pressing his jacket to her chest to staunch the blood, Renee Reading managed to slip away.

There had been no records in her office that gave them any insight into where she'd disappeared. The six children in the semi-trailer that day were returned to either their families or Child Protective Services. Two were able to give them enough information to lead to another raid, resulting in ten more children being rescued. Four adults had been arrested and charged with sex trafficking.

Without her asking – reminding her of how often Hardy called her hard-headed stubborn - she was informed he'd requested personal time and wasn't due back for another week. His supervisor thanked her for her involvement in the assignment and mentioned Hardy had written up a commendation for her file.

"This Hardy," Joyce began when they were alone. That was as far as she got before Shea gave in and let the tears come. Her mother's arms came around her, held and rocked as she emptied her heart of the loss.

On the day of her discharge she turned from packing her few things into a tote at the knock on her door. Shock held her frozen at the sight of Hardy. There was longing as well, but that she quickly buried in temper.

"Made it just in time," she shot out, thrilled that

her voice carried an edge. "Or you're too early, depending on your point of view."

"I need you to come with me."

"Too bad, since I no longer care about what you need." She turned back to her tote.

"I called in a favor and asked a friend to fly us to Tucson."

"You expect me to believe you'd call in a favor? Not the Sinclair I know, the one who refused to do anything that would come anywhere close to his father's behavior."

"I've done nothing but call in favors since I knew you would be okay. When we get there, you'll understand why I haven't been here with you."

She closed her eyes, knowing she was already weakening. Love surpassed anger and hurt. "My parents are taking me home to San Antonio."

"I'll take you there afterward." He cleared his throat. "If that's what you want."

She didn't know how Hardy cleared the trip with her parents, she didn't ask. She also didn't speak during the trip to the airfield. Once the small Cessna lifted off, she kept her seat belt secured and fell asleep. It was the warmth of his hand on her arm that woke her, a warmth she remembered all too well. She continued to hold silent as he drove them into town, and through the campus of the University of Arizona until he parked in front of the Fine Arts Library.

"Wait," he said, exiting and hurrying around the hood fast enough that he opened her door before she could. She lifted her face to the heat of the sun, hoping it would chase away the annoyance of her fatigue.

She followed him inside, down a flight of stairs, through several corridors until they stopped outside what was designated as the faculty conference room. She hated how fatigued the short trip left her. Hardy opened the door, then stepped back to allow her entry. Puzzled, but still too stubborn to ask him anything, she entered.

A man stood staring out the window. He wore khaki slacks and a long-sleeve denim shirt, both of which were loose on a thin frame. When he turned she noted the strands of gray and the lines that scored his features. But it was the eyes that had her heart suddenly pounding. The eyes her brother had also inherited from their mother.

"Joey?" She blinked furiously at the sudden tears. No way would she let anything blur this first look at her brother in more years than she could count.

"Hey, Bossy," he said, calling her the nickname

he claimed she'd earned at age six when she began telling him what to do. "Your friend there knows someone, who knows someone, who knows my handler."

She lifted a hand to rub at her temple. She wanted to go to him, wrap around him. Only he looked so unsure. She supposed the years apart – and the reason for them – was to blame. "Handler?"

Hardy stepped forward, wrapped an arm around her shoulder to guide her to a chair. "You need to sit."

Joey sat next to her. "My handler," he verified. "I'm in witness protection. I've done a lot of shit that I'm not proud of, Shea. You know, you know how that stuff got a hold of me. I just couldn't seem to shake it off." He looked away. She closed her hand over his on his thigh.

"It looks like you did."

"Four years, ten months, and twelve days I've been clean."

"I'm so proud of you."

"You wouldn't have been." He looked at her and his eyes were dark and tormented. "Even as low as I went though there were some things I just wouldn't do. So, when my dealer told me he wouldn't give me any more supply unless I found him some kids." Joey hunched his shoulders. "Kids for the sex trade and they couldn't be more than ten years old." She flicked a glance at Hardy, who stood with his back to them, giving them a measure of privacy.

"If I didn't get him the kids," Joey continued. "He'd make sure I paid. He had people wanting those kids and he'd make sure they knew I was the one who failed. Then they'd mess me up. Even in my scrambled up brain, I knew what that meant. I don't know, something just snapped. And the people he talked about? He gave me names, hoping, I guess, that it would scare me. It did." He got up, went over to tap water into a paper cup, drank deeply and then came back to sit beside her.

"Nothing good happened to anyone who crossed those people. So, I got hold of this cop I knew. He'd been decent to me a couple of times when I got busted. Anyway, I told him what they expected of me. I gave him the names I knew, found out a couple more for him. He sat with me while I came down, held me when I shook with chills, listened when I yelled at him, begged him for a hit. He never left me." Joey lifted his hand, rubbed it over his face. "And when I was finally clean, he gave me a new chance. I got a new name, I'm Adam now, Adam O'Reilly. They moved me, got me the job here. I go to meetings." He smiled a little. "I have a girlfriend."

Shea lifted a hand and brushed it over his shoulder. "Tell me about her."

He talked about how they'd met. She was a single mother of a three-year-old girl and worked in the faculty cafeteria. They talked for almost an hour, with Shea telling him of their parents. Hardy never budged.

"You know you can't tell Mom and Dad," Joey said toward the end of their conversation. "I won't take the chance of someone hurting them because I put them away." He plucked at the sleeves of his shirt and she figured he used the long sleeves to hide the marks of his past.

"I didn't want to talk to you." Now he flicked a look toward Hardy. "But I was promised no one would find out. That you'd be safe."

"So, this is it?" Shea asked, new tears burning her eyes, clogging her throat. She saw the tears in his eyes as well, knew this wasn't any easier on him. His thin arms held her as she buried her face against his chest.

It was hard to let him go, to sit and watch him walk out the door. At least her heart was eased by the knowledge that he was safe and happy. Somehow she'd find a way to tell her parents.

"Thank you," she said. "I don't know how I'll ever repay . . ." Hardy swung around so quickly she jumped a little, wincing at the pull in her shoulder.

"There's nothing to repay."

"There is for me. Do you think I don't know what it cost you to look beyond your own code of conduct and pull whatever strings you had to pull so I could see my brother?" Her breath hitched. "So I could know he's safe."

"What it cost me? A few phone calls?" He took a step toward her. "You took a bullet for me."

"Of course I did, you ass. I love you."

Of all the reactions or responses she might have imagined, never would she have pictured Hardy sinking to his knees. He stared at her and she took her first really hard look at him.

His eyes were bloodshot, his hair looked as if it had been combed with a rake and he had a mustard stain on his shirt.

"I was so pissed at you," she said, ignoring how she found that stain so endearing for some strange reason. "You shut me out. So I thought, what the hell, if that's the way he wants to play it, I'll do my own work. Done it before, can do it again. So I went back to the trucking operation. I saw the trailer rig and something just clicked." She shook her head. "I had no idea Renee was involved. She was taking me to her office when you showed up with Chad."

"He'd called me, wanted to make a deal. I thought you'd be safer if I kept you out of the loop."

"That's weak and you know it. I'm a trained agent, the same as you. If I had been informed, I'd have discussed it with you." She deliberately lifted a hand to rub where she'd been shot.

"Chad had been recruited by Renee a few years ago when they met at a party," Hardy explained. "At first he enjoyed the perks. Her. Then, she kept wanting younger and younger kids. He'd been trying to convince her to stop the business. She laughed, explained she'd been one of those kids once upon a time and she'd been smart enough to make it work for her. No reason these kids couldn't do the same."

"God, she makes me sick."

"We haven't been able to locate her. From what we've learned from some of the people we did manage to round up and question, her network is far and wide with some high profile clients." He stood, moved to the chair beside hers. "We're going after her. A task force, combining forces of both FBI and DEA, has been formed to continue work on uncovering other sites and methods for sex trafficking." Tentatively he reached for her hand. "I've been assigned as Special Agent in Charge."

Her heart began to hammer in her chest. "Congratulations."

"I'd like you to be a part of the team. My team." He lifted her hand, pressed it to his lips. "God, Shea, my heart stopped cold when you were shot. I called the hospital every day, often multiple times. Even when I knew you were going to be okay, all I could think was I'd never told you what you meant to me. Not just the job. I never told you that I need you in my life." He looked at her over their joined hands. "I never told you I love you."

With care he drew her close, kissed her. "Come to Denver with me, Shea. Work with me." His mouth touched hers, moved over to nip at the spot beneath her earlobe, a spot he well knew did it for her every time. "Be with me."

She pressed her forehead to his as she sniffed back tears. "I love you, Hardy. But if you try to shut me out again, I'll hurt you."

"Never again," he promised. "I don't ever want to be without you again. Together, Shea. We'll work together. Love together." His grin flashed, fast and loving as he eased away. "I can't promise the same kind of lifestyle we had while we were undercover, but I can give you this."

She glanced down to see the ring she'd worn while pretending to be his wife.

Her breath lodged in her throat, making it necessary to swallow twice before she could speak. "Please tell me you didn't call in more favors."

"No. I bought it outright from the jeweler the agency used." He shrugged. "I wasn't able to swing the necklace."

"It was heavy anyway."

"It's Valentine's Day. You're not going to break my heart on this day above all others, are you?"

"I guess I lost track of time," she said, immediately regretting the words when his eyes darkened. "I'm fine, Hardy."

"I want to make sure you're always safe." His gaze lightened a little. "Even knowing you're too stubborn and hard-headed for your own good."

Her eyes narrowed. "You might want to rethink those words."

"I trust you to understand what I mean. But just in case, let me say it this way." He leaned forward and lightly kissed her. "Will you wear the ring, my ring this time, Shea? Will you wear it as a favor to me, for real rather than as a prop for the assignment?"

"As your partner? With no evasions or attempts to protect me?"

"I can't." He shook his head. "I'll always want to protect you. But, I can promise you I want to share my life with you. Even the bad parts. As my wife. As the love of my life. In every way possible."

She held out her hand, felt warmth flood her entire body as she stared into his eyes. The warmth came from him, from believing he accepted her as she was and knowing she did the same for him. From knowing they'd have a lifetime together.

"I can't think of anything I want more."

COURTING JULIET

Courting
JULIET

Pam Mantovani

An hour later, Juliet ventured outside. A call to Sadie had confirmed Walker Grant was who he claimed. She'd also vouched for his honor. Since Sadie had her own experience dealing with a stalker, Juliet had agreed with her point that having Walker around the ranch would put her mind at ease.

With the roof of the back porch shielding her from the sun, Juliet paused. The sky was incredibly bright and blue with only a few cotton tuffs of clouds. It was so quiet, nothing at all like the constant drum of traffic and noise she was used to in New York.

She'd come to Montana to escape a monster. And while Walker Grant had been a surprise, a very attractive one, she'd also come here to work and live. Living here meant getting to know people. Trusting them. Time to start. She'd allowed one man to force her into running. She wouldn't allow another.

Stepping off the back porch, she crossed the yard. At the open barn door she paused. The interior might be brighter than she expected, but even her city nose picked up the scents of hay and manure. It hit her then just how truly she'd left the city behind. And hopefully the man who'd terrorized her the past year.

As she studied the interior, she saw there were three stalls on the right side and two on the left. At the end of the wide aisle, on the left at the rear of the barn, there appeared to be a room of some sort. She could hear murmuring, a low comforting tone that brought to mind whispered conversations in bed.

Something brushed her leg just as she took a step forward. Jumping a little at the unexpected sensation, she looked down, her hammering heart going still. "Well, hello." She crouched and ran a hand over the back of the ginger-colored cat. A few strokes later she discovered a heavy belly.

"That's Molly."

Juliet looked up to see Walker approach. She took note that he kept space between them. The way he also kept his hands in the front pockets of his jeans meant she had an unobstructed view of his cock. She shivered a little, speculating how it would feel to be pressed against him. Walker took a miniscule step in retreat.

"She'll be giving you some more barn cats in a few weeks."

"Barn cats?"

"They live out here, keeping mice away." He smiled a little. "The horses seem to like having them around."

"Pet pals." She chuckled at her bad joke. With one last stroke of the cat, she stood.

He may have taken a small step away but they were still standing close. Closer than she'd wanted to be with any man other than her father for far longer than she could recall. Walker kept his gaze steady on hers, his brown eyes filled with interest. His lips were firm and she couldn't help but wonder how they would feel on hers. And anywhere else he might like to linger.

And oh wasn't it glorious to see interest in a man's eyes rather than obsession in a crazed man's gaze?

"Do you have time to give me a tour of my barn?"

"You're the boss."

"Oh, I don't think so. At least not in this arena." She pointed a finger at her chest, felt the heat of a thrill zip through her when his gaze lowered to take in the gesture. "City girl, remember?" His gaze rose and she once again found herself pinned by the intensity of his eyes.

He didn't look much like a ranch hand at the moment. With broad shoulders and strong chest muscles a flannel shirt couldn't disguise he looked like the kind of man you could depend on, the kind of man who would honor his promises and defend you against an enemy.

The romantic part of her heart that never lost hope of finding a lifelong partner sighed with pleasure.

She turned and headed to the first stall where a majestic black horse stood.

"This is Scotty," Walker said as he came to a stop beside her.

Juliet took in the elegant, regal way the horse held his head. "That sounds much too pedestrian a name for such a beauty." She grinned when the horse lowered his head a little in agreement. "Looks like he agrees with me."

"Oh, our Scotty thinks highly of himself."

"How could he not? I might be from the city but even I recognize a magnificent animal when I see one." In the silence that followed, she realized how her comment could be taken. She felt heat flood her cheeks. "What I mean is . . . "

"I know what you mean." Chuckling, he lifted his free hand to scratch at the horse's forehead. At least she thought that was what it was called. Walker shifted to look at her, his brown eyes warm and clear, an enticing invitation to move closer and feel that hand stroke down her back.

When she realized she'd been about to lean into him, she cleared her throat. "You mentioned someone wants to breed their horse with mine?"

"Yes, Avery Sawyer. She and her husband are your neighbors."

"I'm going to guess they're a little further away than the apartment across the hall that I'm used to."

He smiled and gestured her toward another stall. "Avery's ranch is little more than five miles to the west."

"Five miles. And this morning I sent Momma a photo of an elk in my front yard." She shook her head. "My life has taken a drastic turn. Now, who is this?" This horse was a light caramel color in contrast to the darkness of the first, but no less imposing.

"This is Captain."

"Captain," she repeated. She glanced around. "These are the only two?"

"So far." He nodded toward the empty stalls. "You have room to add more. Plenty of pasture for grazing. You could build yourself a tidy little stud service here."

She choked at the suggestion. From the corner of her eye, because God she could not look at him, she saw his lips curve in a grin. Crossing the wide aisle she trailed a fingertip along the leather strap of some sort hanging from another stall. Another reminder of how her life had changed. She hoped, prayed, she'd left more than family and city life behind. She wanted to be able to enjoy living here, trying new experiences. Not being afraid of having an unbalanced man threatening her.

"So, instead of being a horse whisperer, I'll be a horse madam."

He chuckled as he approached to stand beside her. "That's one hell of a way to look at it. But, yeah, I guess you could say that." He shifted so he leaned his left arm on top of the stall's half door and faced her.

"I can handle the stud services for you."

ACKNOWLEDGMENTS

As always I appreciate and am indebted to Elle James. Her unrelenting support and encouragement is valuable beyond words.

For Christine, who not only is a terrific critique partner, always shares valuable information and above all else is a cherished friend, as well as the best darn blurb writer on the planet.

Always and forever, to Denny who shows me that true romance, the kind that lasts a lifetime, is built on all the small thoughts, words and gestures you show me every day.

To the readers who continue to follow and support my writing. Thank you doesn't even begin to say how much I appreciate all of you.

BAREFOOT BAY

HOT SUMMER KISSES

https://bit.ly/2xnH2u4

<u>THE PILOT'S PROMISE</u>

https://bit.ly/2D58zGv

WILD ROSE PRESS

COURTING THE COACH

http://amzn.to/2k88Xu6

SHARED SECRETS

http://amzn.to/29reioM

CRYSTAL CLEAR

http://amzn.to/2kNsYW9

BROTHERHOOD PROTECTORS

ORIGINAL SERIES BY ELLE JAMES

Brotherhood Protectors Series

Montana SEAL (#1)

Bride Protector SEAL (#2)

Montana D-Force (#3)

Cowboy D-Force (#4)

Montana Ranger (#5)

Montana Dog Soldier (#6)

Montana SEAL Daddy (#7)

Montana Ranger's Wedding Vow (#8)

Montana SEAL Undercover Daddy (#9)

Cape Cod SEAL Rescue (#10)

Montana SEAL Friendly Fire (#11)

Montana SEAL's Mail-Order Bride (#12)

SEAL Justice (#13)

Ranger Creed (#14)

Delta Force Strong (#15)

Montana Rescue (Sleeper SEAL)

Hot SEAL Salty Dog (SEALs in Paradise)

Hot SEAL Hawaiian Nights (SEALs in Paradise)

ABOUT ELLE JAMES

ELLE JAMES also writing as MYLA JACKSON is a *New York Times* and *USA Today* Bestselling author of books including cowboys, intrigues and paranormal adventures that keep her readers on the edges of their seats. With over eighty works in a variety of sub-genres and lengths she has published with Harlequin, Samhain, Ellora's Cave, Kensington, Cleis Press, and Avon. When she's not at her computer, she's traveling, snow skiing, boating, or riding her ATV, dreaming up new stories. Learn more about Elle James at www.elle-james.com

Website | Facebook | Twitter | GoodReads | Newsletter | BookBub | Amazon

Follow Elle!
www.ellejames.com
ellejames@ellejames.com

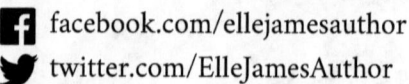
facebook.com/ellejamesauthor
twitter.com/ElleJamesAuthor

www.ingramcontent.com/pod-product-compliance
Lightning Source LLC
Chambersburg PA
CBHW071257130626
46556CB00003B/1357